Eden's Wish

Eden's Wish

M. Tara Crowl

DISNEY • HYPERION
LOS ANGELES   NEW YORK

First Edition, September 2015
1 3 5 7 9 10 8 6 4 2
G475-5664-5-15258

Printed in the United States of America
This book is set in Cochin
Designed by Whitney Manger

ISBN 978-1-4847-1185-9
Library of Congress Control Number: 2015016314

Reinforced binding

Visit www.disneybooks.com

For Adelyn Belle

Eden's Wish

One

On the night when he found the lamp, Darryl Dolan was in a rotten mood.

He'd lost a hundred dollars on a game of pool. Even worse, he'd lost it to a scrawny teenager with thick-framed glasses and peach fuzz.

The kid's friends had egged him on: "Take him, Timmy! Show the old man what you've got!" No one named Timmy ever won a game of pool, Darryl's mate Clyde had said to him confidentially, and Darryl couldn't argue. So he'd raised the stakes from fifty dollars to a hundred. But things didn't go as planned. Darryl pocketed solids with the force of a bulldozer, while Timmy tapped his striped balls feebly. Yet somehow, Timmy managed to end a five-shot streak by sinking the eight ball and winning the game.

It was no surprise, really. Unfortunate things were

always happening to Darryl. The truth was, he was very, very unlucky.

But that night, something unusual happened: in an instant, Darryl's luck *changed*.

As he walked home, a metallic glint caught his eye and drew it to an antique-looking oil lamp. It was wedged between the branches of an overgrown shrub. Without a thought, he reached in and plucked it out.

It was slightly larger than his hand, with a round base and a long spout for pouring. It was old and tarnished—not as flashy a find as he might have liked. Still, with a bit of polishing, it could probably be pawned.

Back in the dirty laundry–scented comfort of his apartment, he located the stained cloth meant for drying dishes in the kitchen. He shoved a plate of crusty remains from Tuesday's breakfast off the couch, sat, and took the cloth to the lamp.

Quick and hot as a bullet, a cracking flash of light knocked the sense right out of Darryl and sent his brain spinning.

He'd never experienced anything like it. Surely, he was dying. This was death.

But when he came to, he was still on the couch. He blinked three times to restore reality.

The first thing he saw was the girl.

She wore a thick white cotton nightgown that tried

to reach her wrists and ankles but faltered, exposing skinny shins and forearms. Three thin pink ribbons encircled her waist. Around one wrist was a thick gold cuff bracelet.

The girl's hair fell to her waist in tangles and sleep-rumpled waves. As he watched, she took in her surroundings: the plaid flannel couch sprinkled with sandwich crumbs, the faded dartboard on the wall. Her eyes traveled over Darryl, judging his faded black T-shirt, thinning hair, and stubborn potbelly. Her lips formed a pout. She crossed her arms and faced him.

"The legends are true—you get three wishes." She spoke rat-a-tat fast and her tone was matter-of-fact. "But there are rules. These are the rules:

"One: Every person has a lifetime limit of three wishes. If by some miracle a mortal happens to find the lamp more than once, the rub won't work. You can't wish for more wishes, and you can't wish for this rule (or any others) to change. That's why they're called the rules.

"Two: You can't change anything from the past. All wishes have to be for the present or the future. So you can't bring a dead person back to life, erase a war, or take back something stupid you said.

"Three: Wording counts. Don't assume you'll get what you want—you'll get what you ask for."

"Wishes?" Darryl frowned. "Are those before the afterlife or in heaven itself? Once I get there, assuming—well, you know. It's all up to you, I suppose."

"Heaven? What are you talking about?" The girl's eyes glittered.

"Well, you're the angel who decides, I suppose? Or will that be another one?"

"Angel? Have you ever heard of an angel coming out of a lamp?"

Darryl paused. Now that he thought about it, he couldn't recall anything happening that would have killed him. "But ... then what *are* you?"

The girl huffed. "I'm a genie, dummy! Lamp, three wishes—how much more do you need?"

Darryl had no answer. She let out an exasperated sigh and spoke slowly, as if to a child: "My name is Eden, and your wish is my command."

In a moment of clarity, Darryl noted that her hair was precisely the color of banana pudding.

"What's this?" She'd appeared at the wall to his left and was examining his weathered dartboard. She touched the soft cork with her finger.

"Dartboard?" Darryl's voice was high and hoarse. He looked on helplessly as she poked the tan and black stripes fanning out from the middle, the red and green bands cutting through them, the winking green iris, and the tough red bull's-eye.

"What are these numbers for?"

"Uh—scoring, of course." He cleared his throat. "Now, you say I have three wishes—"

"You got it, buddy." Eden's fingers locked on one of the darts. It was lodged on the outer edge of the board from Darryl and Clyde's last game. Must have been Clyde's shot, Darryl thought.

With a tug she removed the dart and tested the point on her finger. She turned to Darryl with delight. "Sharp!"

"A bit dangerous, really." Darryl scooted down the couch. "So, for my first wish."

Eden took a few steps back, reared back, and hurled the dart. Ignoring its intended target, it curved to the left and embedded itself in the wall so close to Darryl's head, the breeze tickled the skin under his hair.

"Hey!" he cried, leaping up. "You throw the darts *into* the board, you hear me?"

But she'd already retrieved a second dart and was rearing back again. This one zoomed skyward and burrowed into the ceiling's surface.

"Oops!" She giggled, covering her mouth with her hand.

"You. Have. Horrible aim!" Darryl plucked the third dart from the board before she could reach it. He folded his hand over it. "No more darts for you."

She set her bare feet wider, crossed her arms, and

stuck out her lip. "One more dart, then we'll start the wishes."

"Wishes, *then* dart."

Her pout grew fiercer.

Would he lose the wishes if he didn't do what she ordered? Being an unlucky man, Darryl didn't want to take the chance. He groaned and extended his open hand. Glee flashed on her face as she snatched the dart. She dipped one knee low and wound up like a pitcher on the mound.

"Now just one second—" Darryl started, but it was too late. The moment it escaped her grip, the dart made a beeline for the window to the right. When it hit, the brittle pane of glass burst into a thousand pieces that danced across the living room floor.

Darryl's hands balled into fists. But she was grinning like a child in her first snowfall.

"*Spectacular,*" she breathed.

"You listen to me!" Darryl seethed. "Enough funny stuff. You give me my wishes and then you GET OUT!"

Jolted from her reverie, Eden slouched and rolled her eyes. "Whatever. It's not like I want to hang out in this dump anyway."

Darryl set his shoulders and lifted his chin. "Are you ready for my first wish?"

"Born ready."

He cleared his throat importantly. "I wish to win . . . *the lotto.*"

To his surprise, she laughed. "That," she said, "is exactly what I thought you might say." She held out a thin arm and snapped her fingers. When she did, her bracelet gave a quick pulse of light. A piece of paper, smaller than a postcard, floated down from the heavens. It sailed gently, one way and then the other.

"I've got it! I've got it!" Grasping the card, he yanked it into sight. It was an unscratched lottery scratch card.

"A coin! Have you got a coin?" Eden held up her hands to show they were empty. He sucked in a ragged breath and scrambled to the kitchen, fumbling through the junk drawer. "Crap—where's it—got to be—I swear—ah!" There, under the masses of aspirin, pens, and bottle openers, was a ten-cent coin. Now where had he left that ticket? He sprinted back to the living room, retrieved it from the coffee table, and attacked the scratch section with the coin, digging madly for the promised treasure.

The silver latex flaked off in clumpy bits until the number underneath was revealed.

For a moment Darryl Dolan forgot how to speak. Then he remembered—and exploded.

"FIVE FLIPPIN' DOLLARS???"

The words died unheard in the empty room. The girl had disappeared.

Frantically Darryl surveyed the apartment, but she was gone. Not in the living room, not in the kitchen, not in the hallway that led to his bedroom. But then he looked through the hole in the wall where the window had been, and saw a small white-clad figure on the sidewalk. The girl stood motionless, nightgown swishing in the winter wind. Her face was turned toward the moon.

He stuck his head through the hole. *"Get back in here!"* he hissed. Reluctantly the girl climbed back through the window hole, one willowy leg at a time.

He held up the scratch card for her to see. "WHAT KIND OF RUBBISH GENIE ARE YOU ANYWAY??"

Was that a mischievous smile playing on her lips? "Okay, look," she said. "I told you earlier. Wording counts."

"WHAT?"

"Rule number three. 'Wording counts. Don't assume you'll get what you want—you'll get what you ask for.'" She shrugged. "If you wanted to win the big-time lotto, you should have said so."

A current of despair washed over Darryl. It was like he was back at school, outsmarted by a test's trick question. Here he was, forty years old, and nothing had changed. His shoulders slumped forward. "All my life, an unlucky man."

"Say what?"

"Nothing."

Eden scrutinized him. "What's your name?"

"Darryl."

"Well, Darryl, why don't you think about something you like? Something that makes you really happy. Can you think of something like that?"

A sense of epiphany came over Darryl. "*Yes.*"

"Good. Now put into words precisely what the wish is. If it's money you want, seeing as JUST wishing to win the lottery didn't get you the results you had in mind, if you were to say the *amount* you wanted to win—"

"I wish for an unlimited lifetime supply of hot chips." The words came in a rapid stream.

Eden's pale eyebrows jumped to attention. "Hot chips?"

"Yeah."

Her eyes rolled upward as if searching for something deep in her brain. "We're in Australia, right?"

"Wagga Wagga, Australia, if you want to be exact."

"So when you say hot chips, you mean fried potatoes?"

"Hot chips. Like the ones at the pub."

Eden let out a low whistle and smiled. "Here we go," she said as she raised a hand for her second snap.

The glorious smell of hot grease thickened the air. It seeped through Darryl's nostrils and into his consciousness like a savory sedative. His eyes closed as a stream of pleasant feelings worked its way through his brain. He'd never been warmer, safer, or more content. Though he was standing up, he started to slip into a slow, gorgeous sleep. He'd just eat a few first...

But then Darryl realized that he couldn't move his arms.

Startled from his semi-sedated state, he realized why the smell was so overpowering. *He was packed in a room of hot chips, from the bottom of his feet to the base of his neck!* Every inch of the apartment was absolutely stuffed with them!

"Help!" he shrieked. Again he tried to move his limbs, but it was no good; they were packed in tight. "Help!!"

A few feet in front of him, the iridescent sheen of oil gleamed and a patch of chips rippled. Like a steaming sea monster, Eden surfaced with a sputter. Her hair was plastered to her head in greasy clumps, but her face shone with joy.

"How's this for a lifetime supply?" Her arms shot out of the pit, sending hot chips flying. "Hey, do you know how to backstroke?" Kicking her legs to the surface, she lay back and wheeled her arms wildly.

"This isn't funny!" Darryl wailed. "I didn't want them all at once!"

"Well, why didn't you say so?" Cheerfully she popped a chip in her mouth and chewed. Darryl's head dropped in defeat, and for a moment, she looked almost sorry. "It's going to be fine, Darryl. Look, we'll share the wealth with the neighbors. If we can just push some of them out of that open window—"

"The window *you* broke!"

"Yes, the window I broke!" The pitch of her voice rose, and Darryl shrank away. "Aren't you happy it's broken now? How else would we get out of here?"

"Can't you fix it?"

"The window?"

"THE SITUATION!"

"You have a wish left. *You* fix it!"

Darryl thought very hard for a moment. "Fine!" he said in a burst of inspiration. "I wish for a mansion to fit all these chips!"

Eden winked. "Coming right up!" She held her hand high above the hot mass of chips and snapped for the third time.

Darryl's apartment gave a momentous shudder. Slowly, the walls began to push outward. They grew taller, lifting the ceiling. A grand spiral staircase plunked down in the entryway. Windows planted like seeds in the walls and blossomed to enormous proportions.

The apartment was swelling to two, three, four times its original size. And yet, the level of chips *wasn't going down*. On the contrary, they were multiplying. They churned furiously between the walls, and Darryl fought for air as he churned along with them.

Across the massive mixing bowl, he spotted Eden. Like him, she was treading chips to keep afloat. Unlike him, she was shrieking with happiness.

"What's gone wrong now?" Darryl moaned. "I thought they would fit in a mansion!"

"You asked for an unlimited lifetime supply!!" she shouted. "No matter how big the house is, the chips will fill it! Isn't it fantastic?"

And with that, the churning and shaking halted; the mansion was complete. Her wishes granted, the genie vanished.

Darryl took in the scene. He was a solitary goldfish in a tank full of thick-cut fried potatoes. Really, it was fitting. The first stroke of luck in his life, and it had taken the unluckiest turn you could imagine.

He extracted a chip and ate it. It was delicious. And in that, at least, he was fortunate; he'd be eating them for quite some time.

Two

"Sit," Xavier commanded.

She snapped her eyes closed and concentrated, burying precious stolen moments from Earth in her mind: cool air raising goose bumps on her skin; that inky-black night sky, infinite enough to drown in. She bottled them and stored them in her memory with the others. These moments were her salvation; thanks to them, she was able to endure endless hours in the lamp.

"Look at me, Eden. Look at me and sit."

She opened her eyes. "We've *got* to get a dartboard." She exhaled and collapsed on the stiff-backed chair.

She was back in the lamp, of course. When a granting ended, she always wound up here. She had no choice in the matter.

The lamp's study was her reentry point. The study was a cavern of rare and ancient books stacked on shelves that rose to the ceiling. The rest of the lamp had three levels, but the study wasn't divided into stories; its floor was the ground floor, and its ceiling was at the top of the third floor. It was a skyscraper of a room tucked at the edge of the lamp.

The study was the lamp's only room that she was forbidden to enter unless invited. It was also Xavier's favorite room. He spent lots of time there, and kept it in impeccable order.

As was their custom, Xavier and Goldie were sitting at their desks: grand, ornately carved pieces made of walnut. Unlike the one Eden sat in, their chairs were plush and covered with leather. Xavier's was forest green; Goldie's was crimson.

Behind them was a towering set of drawers that curved with the belly of the lamp. Between the two desks, a regal telescope balanced on three slender legs.

In the dimly lit air, particles of dust floated like tiny fragments of knowledge. The volumes were pushed tightly against one another, with not an inch of shelf space to spare.

They needed to breathe, Eden thought. She knew the feeling.

Xavier set his elbows on his desk and peered at her through his eyeglasses like she was a specimen under a microscope. He was tall and broad-shouldered, with dark hair that he slicked back and parted on one side. Once, on a granting in Mumbai, the wisher's wife had been watching a movie on a rabbit-eared television. Eden had gaped at the man on-screen; surely it was him. The resemblance was uncanny. Though the actor's skin was more tanned than a lamp dweller's could ever be, the amused eyes, thin mustache, and self-assured swagger were nearly identical. In the wisher's dialect she'd breathlessly asked who he was. "Rhett Butler," the woman had answered. "Haven't you ever seen *Gone with the Wind*?"

Next to him, Goldie was eying Eden with concern. Goldie was pretty, plump, and pink-cheeked, with kind eyes and a tiny perfect nose. As a rule, she was more indulgent than Xavier, but over the years Eden had learned that crossing her wasn't wise.

"Eden," Xavier said, "what is your assessment of today's granting?"

Honestly, she thought it had gone quite well. Even though the summons had awoken her rudely in the middle of the night, some good had come of it. She'd seen four constellations: Orion, Canis Major, Aries, and Gemini. She'd discovered a new game. She'd gone for a swim—well, sort of a swim. And along the way, she'd taught a valuable lesson to a foolish wisher.

That was her truthful assessment. But she had a feeling the masters of the lamp might not agree.

She willed herself not to break eye contact. "I think it went well. Pretty standard."

Goldie winced. A muscle in Xavier's jaw twitched. *"Pretty standard.* Do you really think that's true?"

She bit her lower lip. Xavier never lost his temper. When he was angry, he just got smarter. And he was very, very smart to begin with.

"Eden, you left that poor man smothered by hot chips in a preposterously large house, with a scratch-off ticket buried somewhere underneath entitling him to a five-dollar prize."

Eden looked down at the gold cuff bracelet on her right wrist. Her name was etched across it in cursive. When she was granting a wish, light shone through the lines of the letters. When the letters were shining, the lamp's magic was active. Xavier and Goldie each wore an identical bracelet, but with their own names, of course.

Eden caught the elastic band of her nightgown sleeve's cuff between her fingers and tugged it down over the bracelet.

"The man has no choice but to, for lack of a more eloquent phrase, eat his way to freedom. If—and that is, *if*—he makes it out alive, he'll find that his new residence has encroached upon the property of his neighbors and damaged their dwellings. His peers will berate him. He may never succeed in removing the scent of grease from his person. All this only if he manages to emerge from the house without suffering congestive heart failure."

Xavier leaned forward. "That was not *'pretty standard.'*" His voice lowered to a whisper but retained its force, like a giant stooping to average height. "Do you see what I mean?"

Eden steeled herself. "He got what he asked for," she said. "You two taught me the rules."

"Eden—"

"Number three: wording counts. Goldie, you taught me that."

"Eden, we've been through this," Goldie said with a sigh. "Those rules exist so wishers don't take advantage of us. Not so that *we* can take advantage of *them.*"

"Of *course* they don't always word things properly," Xavier said. "You've got to remember, these are mortals. They're simple."

"That's for sure," Eden said under her breath.

Xavier blinked. He took off his glasses and massaged the inner corners of his eyes.

"The day after tomorrow, at breakfast."

"*What?*"

Xavier raised his dark, finely shaped eyebrows. "You know how I feel about that tone."

"Fine. *What* will happen the day after tomorrow at breakfast, dear Xavier?"

He ignored the sarcasm. "The day after tomorrow at breakfast you'll hand me a written report on how tonight's granting *should* have been handled."

"A *what?*"

"I expect your best penmanship and no errors in spelling or grammar—"

"You've got to be *kidding* me. This is so—"

"ENOUGH!" The word struck Eden like a slap. "I will *not* have this behavior in my lamp."

Indignation stung Eden's cheeks. She blinked fast so the hot liquid gathering behind her eyes wouldn't spill over.

"Goldie?" she tried.

Eden could tell that Goldie was struggling to stay stern. It didn't come naturally for her.

"You heard Xavier," she said. "There's a way to behave on grantings, and this isn't it."

Xavier smoothed a hand over his hair and closed his eyes as if in pain. For several moments he was silent. Finally he spoke.

"Ours is a *pleasant* business. We grant wishes. We make people *happy.* During your career, you are our representative. You show up, you make someone's dreams come true."

The same spiel she'd heard since her training had begun at age three.

"You are the only person on this planet who can do that. The *only one.* Because you're part of a legacy like no other." His favorite phrase. "And until you complete your lifetime wish quota, you have a *responsibility* to serve each wisher to the best of your ability."

"And what if I don't want to?" The words tumbled from her mouth even though she already knew the answer.

Xavier blinked. The haughty clock ticked on the wall: *clock, clock, clock, clock.*

"You'll do it anyway," he said. And with that, she was sent to bed.

Three

Eden was well aware of the honor of her position. Genies had been granting mortals' wishes for thousands of years. During all that time, no two of them had ever been alike. There'd been wise genies and playful genies, solemn genies and coy genies. Raven-haired genies and pixie-haired genies. Doe-like genies, firecracker genies, foxy genies, and majestic genies.

But there had never been a genie who didn't want to be a genie. Goldie and Xavier had told her so, and they would know. As masters of the lamp, they'd raised every single one.

Sitting sullenly at her vanity, Eden dragged a sapphire-encrusted comb through her hair. Clumps of hot-chip grease had been shampooed away and washed down the shower drain, and now her damp locks felt limp, lacking—what? Spirit, maybe.

She'd spent every night of her life here, in a bedroom

fit for a princess. The chandelier showered a frozen storm of diamonds over a whisper-soft carpet. Delicate cloths of lace and satin adorned the walls. The monstrous closet was populated by gleaming mink coats, elegant dresses, and hundreds of fabulous shoes.

And yet, for her, the room was a prison. The solid gold walls held her captive like an animal in one of the zoos she'd read about. Each night she was doomed to her plush canopy bed, where her head sank into goosedown pillows, and Egyptian cotton sheets clutched at her limbs.

Eden tapped the comb on the nose of her melancholy mirror image, but the girl in the mirror didn't react. She combed a sheet of hair over her eyes so she and the girl wouldn't have to look at each other.

Sometimes she was sure something was wrong with her. Genies were born into service in the lamp. Granting wishes had always been her destiny. So how could she want a different life? Why did she yearn day and night for those blessed escapes from the lamp?

It was a shame she hadn't seen the sun this time. The night sky was thrilling too—so still and sober and endless. But how she loved that fat, brassy sun!

She'd seen it on her very first granting. On a summer morning in a French village called Usson, the wife of a wheat farmer had struck the lamp with her shovel as she dug a new patch for her garden. She unearthed it from the fertile red soil and rubbed it with her apron. In a flash Eden appeared, ten and timid, a baby genie freshly trained.

She'd learned about the sun; she knew its mass (1.9891×10^{30} kilograms), its makeup (approximately three-quarters hydrogen and one-quarter helium), the temperature of its core (approximately 15.7×10^6 °K). She'd seen intimate photos of its undulating surface captured by satellites in space. She'd seen it in photos taken from Earth: high in the sky, an orange glob like an egg yolk, or tucked into the horizon, half swallowed by the sea.

But none of it had prepared her for its glory, for the pulse of those rays reaching desperately to warm her. How could the sun love her so when they'd only just met?

Yet when she sought the rays' source, she staggered backward in pain. Stinging currents shot through her eye sockets. Xavier had warned her to shield her eyes from direct sun, but she couldn't have imagined light like this. She was used to the soft glow of her chandelier and to the flickering of candles on the dining table. Now she saw they were thin imitations of the bright light that baked the Earth like a cake in an oven.

She was so enraptured that she didn't notice the farmer's wife gaping at her like she was a ghost. Tearing her attention from the sky, Eden clumsily granted the woman's wishes (a bountiful spring harvest; a cure for her infant son's colic; a ruby necklace like the one the president's wife had worn in the papers the previous week). But it was hard to concentrate. How could mortals focus with that big, brilliant sun spraying its splendor all over the place?

Genies weren't supposed to be enamored of earthly things. They had to learn about the world, but they weren't meant to share mortals' simple desires. That was what Xavier and Goldie told her in that first post-granting assessment.

But it was too late. From that point forward, her visits were filled with earthly discoveries. Fragrant grass, and sweet or spicy air. Trees. Dirt. Dogs, heavy with age or manic with energy. Rain. Porches—part of the home, yet open to the outside. *Windows*.

Mortals were so jaded that they took these wonders for granted. They snatched at wealth and luxury, gold and jewels, mansions and yachts. And *hot chips*. Well, that had been a new one.

Eden shook her head violently and flipped her hair back so that it rose from her scalp like a lion's mane. She and her reflection locked eyes in the mirror, united and alone in the truth.

The truth was that she was in love with the world. And there's no worse agony than forbidden love.

A gentle rap came at the door. "Come in," Eden said.

Goldie entered the genie's chambers and closed the door softly behind her. She was holding a plate containing a wedge of peach pie. When Goldie entered a room, something delicious usually entered with her. She baked plain old break-your-heart chocolate chip cookies, sticky-sweet maple walnut chews, and peanut butter cookies crowned with careful crosshatches. She baked apple-rhubarb pies, key lime pies, and gooey peach pies. Sometimes she baked a cake: red velvet with cream cheese frosting, or hearty, chunky carrot cake. Considering the lamp's small population, she baked to excess, yet somehow the goods always vanished.

Spotting the grease-soiled nightgown on the floor, Goldie scooped it up for inspection. "Don't think we'll be able to salvage this one. But it was getting small anyway, wasn't it?" Eden shrugged. She had a hundred nightgowns. What did it matter?

Goldie sat on the bed and patted the spot beside her. "Don't talk," she said. "Just eat." Gratefully Eden picked up the fork; until this very moment she hadn't realized how hungry she was. She devoured the slice in huge, gooey bites.

"That's my girl!" Goldie beamed. "There's no cure for a bad granting like warm peach pie. It's done the trick for every one of you girls."

Eden's heel swung back and cracked the wooden bed frame. "Why is Xavier so *mean*?"

Goldie pursed her lips. "Honey, I know he can come off a little harsh. But it's only because he knows you can do better. We want you to live up to your potential."

Eden scoffed. How much potential could you live up to in a prison? Potential lay out there on Earth, not trapped in an antique oil lamp.

She frowned as she tried to stick the remaining piecrust crumbs on the tines of her fork. "Goldie," she said, "are you *sure* I'm supposed to be a genie?"

"Darling, you wouldn't *be* here if you weren't!" Goldie smiled fondly. "Every genie who's ever lived in this lamp was created to grant wishes. That means you were born for something special. Being a genie is your destiny."

"But what if the lamp made a mistake with me?"

Goldie laughed. "Nonsense! The lamp can't make mistakes!" She took Eden's wrist in her hand. "If you're ever unsure of who you are, look at your bracelet and remember." Each resident genie wore the bracelet for the duration of her career. When she retired, the bracelet would be deactivated, and its light would be extinguished forever. At the moment of deactivation, a new bracelet would appear on the wrist of the baby genie born to take her place.

"I know writing the report seems like a drag," Goldie went on. "But you've got to do it. Might as well put on a happy face and make the best of it."

A fresh surge of irritation coursed through Eden's veins. *You've got to do it.* Wasn't that how everything worked around here? Until she granted all her wishes, she couldn't make a single decision for herself.

"Now listen." Goldie took Eden's hands. "No point in getting down after a bad granting. Every genie has them. We use what we've learned to make the next time better. Tomorrow, or the next day, or a week or a month from now, someone new will find the lamp, and you'll grant like a pro." Her eyes flashed. "You'll knock their socks off."

But that was the problem. Eden didn't want to make the next time better. She'd had enough of brief escapes; she wanted to leave the lamp for good. She pulled her hands away from Goldie's and folded her arms across her chest.

"How. About. This." Goldie spaced out her words to build suspense, like she was about to announce something brilliant. "Let's you and me have a girls' sleepover, like we used to. I know you've had a growth spurt, but this bed's still big enough for the two of us! I'll make some hot cocoa and bring us another slice of pie. I've got a chess pie that you'll absolutely—"

"I don't think so," Eden interrupted. Strange how she used to beg for girls' sleepovers with Goldie. These days, the idea had lost its luster. "It's been a long night. I think I'll go to bed."

Disappointment flashed across Goldie's face, but she quickly concealed it. "All right, missy. Next time, I guess. Good night." Empty plate in one hand and soiled nightgown in the other, she kissed Eden on the forehead and left.

At the click of the door, Eden fell back on the bed and let out a slow stream of air. Her eyes drifted to a hazy unfocusedness as she peered into the shimmery folds of the canopy above.

Did she really *have* to write the report? She'd never challenged Xavier or Goldie's commands before. They were the masters; their word was law. But what punishment could Xavier give that would make things worse than they were now?

With a burst of energy she sprang from her snow-angel imprint on the bed. She threw open the closet door, strode to the back, and pushed aside floor-length dresses to expose a section of solid gold wall with a row of maroon-colored marks grouped in threes. She dropped to her knees and picked up the tube of lipstick lying on the floor, a tool pilfered long ago from Goldie. With it she added three ticks, bringing their total to thirty-three. Thirty-three wishes down, 966 to go.

By the time she'd started brushing her baby teeth, Eden had already known her career would consist of 999 wishes. That was the quota for every genie who inhabited the lamp. Since each wisher got three wishes, each genie was summoned 333 times. That could take fifty years, or forty, or maybe, if she was lucky, thirty.

A genie's career began at age ten, so she'd been granting for two and a half years. Eleven escapes from the lamp, ranging from a few minutes to just under an hour. There was no limit on the time a wisher could possess the lamp, but, as Xavier said, mortals were simple; they wished frantically and lustily. As soon as three wishes were granted, Eden was banished back into the lamp, where she was kept safe and sheltered, as hopelessly confined as a songbird in a cage.

After 999 wishes, the genie got her thousandth wish—and that wish was her own. With it, she could choose whatever she wanted for the rest of her life. It all had to be included in a single wish, but after that many grantings, genies were masterful at wording to maximize results.

In the dark of the closet, she shut her eyes. *Maybe this time the lamp will land on a bustling street corner. Mortals will fight for it, and I'll be summoned at any moment. Maybe a little girl just picked it up, and she's rubbing it now*—Eden braced herself for that rocket ride out of the lamp and the lightning-fast growth to a thousand times her current size.

But it didn't come. When would it? When would she see that infinite night sky or greet that brassy sun again?

She shoved the dresses back in place. She'd made up her mind: she wouldn't write the report. And if that tipped the ancient balance of the lamp, so be it. Maybe for once things would get interesting around here.

Four

In the lamp you couldn't see the sun rise or set, so you'd think the time of day wouldn't be important. But with Xavier in charge, that wasn't the case. He commanded an army of clocks stationed in the living room, the kitchen, the lesson room, and the study. Sure as a swinging pendulum, he strode from clock to clock, consulting the fat gold watch on his wrist to ensure they never disagreed with one another.

Every morning at 7:30 A.M., Eden awoke to the sound of Xavier's booming voice belting a show tune. He had perfect pitch and a vast mental catalog of songs. Sometimes he sang "On the Street Where You Live" from *My Fair Lady* or "If I Were a Rich Man" from *Fiddler on the Roof*. Other mornings it was "Almost Like Being in Love" from *Brigadoon* or "Tonight" from *West Side Story*. Often Goldie chimed in, her voice earnest and clear as a bell.

On the morning after the Darryl Dolan granting, the wake-up song was one of his favorites: the opening number of *Oklahoma!*.

"Oh, what a beautiful MORNIN'! Oh, what a beautiful day!"

Eden groaned and pulled the goose-down comforter over her head.

"I've got a beautiful FEELIN', everything's going my way!"

It was no use. She flung the covers aside and swung her bare feet to the carpet. Another day was beginning, and there was nothing she could do about it.

She took a quick shower, braided her hair into a pale rope, and pulled on a long-sleeved cobalt-blue dress. With the exception of her nightclothes, there was no casual attire in the closet.

"Eden!" Xavier's voice bounced off the walls and rang through the lamp just as the clock downstairs chimed 8 A.M. "Breakfast time!" Right on schedule.

"Coming!" she yelled as she clambered down the tight spiral staircase. Sliding down the railing was more fun, but she could only do it when Xavier wasn't watching. She bounded into the dining room and sailed into her seat.

"Pancakes," Goldie said, lowering a steaming stack of them. Maple syrup gleamed down the sides, and a pile of fresh red strawberries sat on top. Eden began tearing into them before the plate touched the table. In the seat across from her, Xavier looked on with amusement.

As she ate, Eden imagined how he'd react when she told him she hadn't written the report he'd assigned. Finally he'd learn he couldn't order her around like a tyrant. The thought made her smile.

At 8:30 A.M., lessons began.

The lesson room where she spent her days was on the second floor across from her bedroom. Unlike the towering study, it was wide and hollow—far too large for a class of one pupil. Large, hexagon-shaped tiles of burgundy and navy stretched across the floor in a sensible pattern, and a dull green chalkboard held court at the head of the room.

Xavier and Goldie said that a genie's education must be classical and comprehensive. In order for the genie to understand the world she granted for, her education had to include history, geography, the sciences, language arts, literature, and art. These earthly subjects were Xavier's domain. He was equally passionate about each, and when he taught, he was in his element. He knew everything. It was difficult to say where and when he'd learned everything one could possibly know, but there was no denying that it was all packed tightly inside his brain. His lectures were jam-packed with facts, and he presented them with theatrical gusto.

The lesson room lacked nothing that could aid a

genie's learning, and the lamp's magic made it all interactive. There was a globe with three-dimensional mountains you could climb with your fingers, and a wide selection of maps could be pulled from a bar above the chalkboard with a snap of the fingers. Eden's favorite map showed constellations that sparkled and twinkled in the dark night sky.

Mahogany bookshelves that rose as high as her chest (so that during a genie's childhood, no book was out of reach) stretched along both sides of the lesson room. They were filled with carefully organized textbooks and novels. Not nearly as many books as there were in the lofty shelves of the study, but enough to provide an answer for every question she'd ever come up with.

On top of the shelves were hands-on learning tools. Most of them were also enchanted, to give them an extra edge. There were magnetic triangles that arranged themselves into various polyhedrons; a model demonstrating the living, pumping inner workings of a human heart; and a chemistry station along the back wall where chemical compounds materialized upon request, ready for experiments. Some things in the lesson room were fun to play with when Xavier wasn't watching: the dinosaur miniatures could fight in pretend prehistoric battles, and the wooden artists' mannequins with movable joints were just asking to do funny dances.

But ultimately, no tool or treasure could change the fact that the lesson room was another ward of her prison. Often she gazed at the poster of the periodic table or at the Van Gogh and Picasso prints on the walls, thinking, If only I had a window! One window! How a small patch of sky would brighten the hours!

Still, she liked learning about Earth. Every piece of information helped her understand the world she loved so much. Some was essential. It was a no-brainer that a genie would need to be fluent in every language; otherwise how could she grant the wishes of a randomly selected person anywhere on Earth? And biology fascinated her—she couldn't get enough of Earth's countless varieties of plants, animals, and insects. She could identify every breed of dog and over a thousand species of trees. Apparently, mortals couldn't retain this much information, but genies were enchanted with the ability to utilize their brains' full capacity.

While Xavier taught the Earth-based curriculum, Goldie handled the genie side of Eden's education. Her courses, Granting for Genies and Lamp History, were taught at the end of each day while Xavier prepared dinner.

The Lamp History course guide, a one-of-a-kind book that Goldie had personally written and illustrated, covered each genie's career and most noteworthy wishes granted. A granting had to have a significant impact on the world to be included in the course guide, so credits were regarded as marks of excellence for the genie.

And there were a lot of them. Most mortals would never know that some of humanity's proudest accomplishments had been enabled by grantings. Countless athletes, musicians, political leaders, and cultural icons owed their skills and positions to the lamp. In fact, so many celebrated figures had rubbed it that it was hard for Eden to believe mortals achieved anything worthwhile on their own.

Years ago, she'd memorized the faces of the genies in the book's portraits. She longed desperately for the day when her own portrait would join them. That would mean she'd reached retirement, and her final escape from the lamp.

Today they were studying Faye, a strawberry blond genie with piercing blue eyes. Her career had spanned from the late 1800s through 1937. Her wishers had included Orville Wright and Jackie Robinson.

While Goldie talked, Eden flipped back the pages of the course guide. Before Faye was Bambi, a genie with thick eyebrows and golden skin. Before her was Julianna, a feisty-looking brunette with a sharp jawline and bright green eyes. The genie before her resembled a full-grown fairy, with very straight silver-blond hair. Her name was Ivy, and she'd granted Beethoven his musical genius.

She turned to the very beginning. The first genie was Athena, a striking woman with caramel-colored skin and close-cropped hair. Her career had begun the lamp's legacy in 2440 BC. Next was Zoe, who had Asian features and a sweet smile. Eden flipped forward through the centuries. She moved quickly past Bola, who'd granted for Julius Caesar. She had dark skin, bright white teeth, and a gaze cold enough to freeze water. For a moment Eden remained in the section on Tabitha, a voluptuous beauty whose grantings were instrumental to the start of the Renaissance. And right after her was Noel, who'd granted for Christopher Columbus. Her dark hair was pulled back in a severe bun, and there was a no-nonsense expression on her face.

But finally, inevitably, Eden reached the place where she always seemed to land: Sylvana's page.

Sylvana was not a recent alum; she'd granted during the Dark Ages. Still, Eden had always felt a mysterious connection to her—more than to any other genie in the book.

Her portrait showed a sly stunner with mischief in her eyes. Her hair was long and honey hued, and one eyebrow was arched in a challenge. Unlike the others, she looked like she had a sense of humor.

But the portrait wasn't what intrigued Eden the most. Years ago, she'd noticed that although Sylvana's career had spanned forty-seven years, her section didn't include a single granting credit. Unlike every other genie in the course guide, only her name and the years of her residence were listed. It seemed she hadn't granted a single noteworthy wish.

Whenever Eden asked about Sylvana, Goldie went strangely silent. "Some genies' careers are more distinguished than others," she'd say. "If you work hard and always try your best, you'll have a list of credits longer than any in this book." As if that were something she'd ever care about.

"So because of Orville Wright's second wish, the world was introduced to flight," Goldie said pleasantly. "One of many wishes brilliantly granted by Faye."

Eden blinked. She'd completely zoned out.

"What's Faye doing now?" she asked. "I've never seen a message from her."

The corners of Goldie's mouth turned down. "You know that's not part of our lesson."

Eden was always trying to find out more about genies' post-lamp lives. Goldie tried to avoid discussing them during lessons, but every once in a while, Eden managed to maneuver her onto the subject.

When a genie retired, she could never enter the lamp again. However, if alumni chose, they could communicate with Xavier and Goldie through a magical mail system. A never-ending roll of enchanted parchment in the study allowed the lamp's masters to record what mortals would call a video (though they'd used it long before that technology existed on Earth). After recording the message, they rolled up the parchment and inserted it into a small circular slot in the wall of drawers behind their desks. From there, the lamp's magic whisked it away into the hands of the alum it was for.

When the alum received it, she could record a response and send it back. When it arrived, it dropped from the slot onto the study floor.

Every so often, they let Eden watch incoming messages—but never before Goldie and Xavier had watched them first.

"Has Nala sent a message back?" Eden asked.

Goldie pursed her lips.

"She did, didn't she?" Eden gripped her desk excitedly. "Oh, please, Goldie, can I see it?"

"Oh..." Goldie wrinkled her nose as she tried to decide.

"Please? I won't ask about any more, I promise."

"Well, all right." Goldie smiled. "It's a short one, anyway."

She left to retrieve the message. They kept them filed in the drawers downstairs.

While she was gone, Eden examined Sylvana's portrait again. She'd never seen a message from Sylvana. What was she like? Funny? Sarcastic? Mischievous? And what was she doing now?

She couldn't have been a very good genie. Otherwise, why wouldn't the course guide mention a single wish she'd granted?

Maybe she'd been like Eden. Maybe she hadn't been sure whether she was meant to be a genie at all.

"I told Xavier I was fetching his copy of the Wright brothers' biography," Goldie said with a giggle. Xavier was much stricter about keeping talk of alumni's retired lives on Earth out of the classroom. Goldie sat next to Eden and unrolled the parchment.

"*Buongiorno* from Capri!" Nala said as the image on the paper came to life. Nala, an alum who'd granted from 1122 to 1188, was tall and slim, with high cheekbones, olive skin, and long black hair. She was lounging in a swimsuit on a small, deserted beach. Behind her was clear blue-green water, with rocky cliffs rising in the background. The sky was bright blue, with puffy white clouds floating by.

"I'm traveling through Italy at the moment! Isn't it beautiful?" She rotated the parchment to show a few quiet cafés and snack bars behind her. "I've just come from Positano. The Amalfi coast is lovely! Good shopping, too." She grinned. "Well, that's all for now! It was great to hear from you guys! You're both looking well! Ciao!" She blew a kiss, and the video ended.

"Wow!" Eden breathed. "Capri! That's the first place I'm going when I finish my lifetime quota."

An uncomfortable silence settled as Goldie rolled up the parchment.

"Or South America." In Rio de Janeiro she'd done a granting for a wide-eyed girl named Jade. "I've *got* to go back to Brazil."

"Someday, dear," Goldie said lightly.

"Goldie, if you could visit Earth again, where would you go first?"

Goldie raised her eyebrows. "Honey, after all these years, you really think I want to go out there in that big ugly world? No, sir! I'm happy right here in paradise."

Eden rolled her eyes. She couldn't understand how you'd want to be inside a stuffy lamp after seeing places like where Nala was. From what Eden could tell, most alumni spent their centuries in endless pursuit of adventure and pleasure—and she fully intended to do the same.

It was strange, though. As far as she knew, all the alumni currently on Earth were immortal. The rare exceptions who'd chosen mortality had died long ago. That meant almost every woman in the course guide should be circulating on Earth. And yet, Eden had seen messages from less than half of them. The others, she couldn't seem to learn a thing about.

"I was wondering. Do you ever hear from Kingsley?" They'd covered Kingsley's career, a fascinating tenure during the reign of ancient Rome. But Eden had no idea what she'd done since 218 BC.

Goldie rolled the parchment back up. "Not for quite some time," she said in a strange, high voice.

"Or Violet?" Violet had come right before Kingsley.

"Violet always kept to herself."

"And what about Sylvana?"

Goldie was suddenly seized by a coughing fit.

"Let me guess. You don't hear from her either?"

Goldie took a deep breath. "Some alumni communicate with us," she said shakily. "Others don't. The choice is theirs."

Eden looked down at Sylvana's portrait again. What would make a genie choose to cut off contact with the lamp?

"Now, where were we? Ah, yes. Orville Wright," Goldie said purposefully, and the lesson resumed.

Five

When the smells of whatever Xavier was cooking for dinner came wafting up the spiral staircase, focusing on lessons became nearly impossible. At last the lesson room clock conceded it was 5 P.M., and Eden was dismissed. She shot downstairs with jet pack power.

"Child, you move like a tornado!" Goldie exclaimed, chasing behind her as she tore into the kitchen. Destruction *did* tend to follow her closely, stepping on her heels if she wasn't careful. Bowls fell off the counter, glasses tipped, and pots boiled over when she whizzed by, though she was sure she couldn't be blamed for the pots.

Dinner was a seafood gumbo, one of Xavier's favorite meals. He had a supernatural tolerance for spiciness, so sometimes he went overboard with the hot sauce.

"Delicious," Goldie pronounced, nudging a tear from her eye with a knuckle. Using her hand to block Xavier's view, she stuck her tongue out to air it. The dining room was even darker than the rest of the lamp, lit only by candles held aloft by a slender silver candelabrum, so you could get away with things like that. Eden gulped ice water to soothe her burning mouth.

Oblivious, Xavier bit into a piece of shrimp large enough to qualify as a fire hazard.

"I have a question," Eden said. "If I can't get hurt, then why is my mouth on fire right now?"

Goldie covered her mouth with a napkin to hide a smile.

"You know this," Xavier said, visibly annoyed. "When Goldie and I became masters of the lamp, we decided that genies should feel pain like mortals. It's important for you to be able to experience things the way they do."

"Maybe you should have thought about that when you were cooking tonight," Eden retorted.

He cleared his throat. "I'm looking forward to reading that report tomorrow morning," he said. "I hope you've started it?"

"Nope!" Eden sang out.

"Well, I guess we know what you're going to be doing after dinner."

"I'm not sure if I'll be able to write it. It's strange, I can't think of much I'd want to do differently."

Xavier took a slow sip of water. "Here's a good place to start. You should never have played with that wisher's darts. You could have seriously injured him. *Always* avoid sharp objects."

She sighed and crossed her arms.

"And I truly hope you don't think treading in a room filled with fried potatoes is the same as swimming. You *must* avoid bodies of water."

"That was a *joke*," Eden muttered.

But Xavier was on a roll. Danger on Earth was one of his favorite topics of conversation.

"While we're on the subject, I must reiterate: whatever you do, *never* get inside a moving vehicle. They're absolute death traps for mortals."

He was *so* melodramatic.

"And although this wasn't the case with the mortal last night, you really *have* to be wary of wishers who try to befriend you. They'll only try to take advantage of your powers."

Sometimes Eden couldn't believe how clueless he was. Each of the eleven mortals she'd granted for had been dumb, but totally harmless. Xavier constantly talked about tragedy: tornadoes and earthquakes, oppression and shame, malaria and AIDS. He said the world was unpredictable and unsafe. But when was the last time he was there anyway? She probably knew more about it than he did!

No matter how he tried to make her fear it, she couldn't stop wishing for the world.

"And finally, always guard your bracelet. As long as each of us is wearing ours, we're safe. If one of them were ever to come off, the lamp's enchantment would be broken, and life as we know it would end." He took a deep breath. "You'd no longer be a genie, which means you'd never get to make a final wish. And as for Goldie and me . . . we're only alive and immortal because of that enchantment. We'd lose our lives instantly."

"I *get* it," Eden said. "Don't take off the bracelet. You've told me a million times." The truth was, she didn't even know *how* to take it off. As far as she could tell, it was locked on tight, with no clasp or opening whatsoever.

Xavier tugged on one side of his mustache. "Eden, this isn't to be taken lightly. Remember, if things go wrong, you can always come home." The lamp's rules allowed a request for reentry in case of emergency. To perform it, she simply had to hold the lamp in front of her and ask to go back inside.

"As if I'd ever sacrifice a moment on Earth."

Goldie gasped. "What a thing to say!"

"It's *true*." Eden drank her water greedily and replaced the empty glass with an unwelcome *thunk*. "I wish I was done being a genie already. All I want is to live out there."

Silence settled on the table like a thick, low-lying cloud. A spoon clinked against a bowl.

"When you've finished your career, you can live any life you choose." Xavier's tongue cut the words into child-size portions. "But while you're in this lamp, you'll grant nine hundred and ninety-nine wishes like every other genie in history. Granting is a *privilege*. You are part of—"

"A legacy like no other. Yeah, yeah, yeah." Eden sighed and pushed around the rice hardening into gummy clumps in her bowl. "Can I be excused?"

"Hm!" said Goldie softly. Her hand rose to smooth her hair, gathered high on her head in a silver-blond bun.

Xavier was glaring at Eden with eyes that burned hot as coals. She narrowed hers right back at him.

"I'm sorry, *may* I be excused?"

The air between them seemed to vibrate. Even the candles flickered in fear.

"If you're finished," Xavier said evenly. "Rinse your dishes in the kitchen."

She flipped her braid, squared her shoulders, and marched out.

She meant to go straight to her room, but instead, after scraping rice and bits of sausage from her bowl into the garbage, she wandered into the living room. In the corner was a very large marble globe with pale green seas and bronze landmasses. It was six feet in diameter and mounted in a solid gold stand, and it stood on a platform elevated two steps above the floor.

As if drawn by a magnetic force, she ascended the steps to the platform and found herself tracing the nations' outlines. She ran a finger round the robust curve of western Africa, then down the snaky tail of Chile. Once she retired and could roam the earth freely, she thought, she'd walk along the coast of every continent. How long would that take? she wondered. Longer than granting 999 wishes? Would a mortal's lifetime be long enough?

The globe was enchanted by the same magic that made the lamp work. When the genie was summoned, it revealed her location. As soon as she disappeared from the lamp—but not a moment before—a gold peg moved to the place where she'd been summoned.

She turned the globe to where the gold peg was affixed to a point in southeast Australia. When the lamp was rubbed again, it would move to the new location where she'd been summoned. After noting its placement, Xavier would advance to his study to observe the granting through the gleaming telescope. Through its lens, he was able to see and hear everything that happened in the lamp's proximity. While she was on Earth, as long as the lamp was near, she could never escape his gaze.

"Do you remember the origin of the word *genie*?" Startled, Eden spun to see Xavier. She hadn't heard him enter, but there he was, straight-backed but at ease in a scarlet armchair across the room. One leg was crossed over the other in a wide authoritative manner. He had a way of making furniture look like it would be incomplete without him.

"Of course." Eden's voice fell flat and weak in the space between them. With one powerful hand he motioned for her to elaborate. "Genie is the English term for the Arabic word *jinn*. It's derived from the root *j-n-n*, which means to hide or conceal."

"That's correct. From the same root, *j-n-n*, Jannah is the Islamic conception of paradise, directly translated as 'garden.'" His eyes searched hers. "I like to think of our home as a paradise. Our own little paradise, where nothing can hurt us."

Eden turned back to the globe and gave it a gentle shove, sending it slowly spinning.

"I know," Xavier said, "that sometimes you feel stifled in the lamp. You think you'd like to get out and explore. Try a different life. Run away, if you could."

Eden kept her back to him. Her eyes ran rapidly over Africa. She felt like the walls were inching inward.

"But darling, I promise you: it doesn't get better than this. Don't you see? You have a life mortals can only dream of."

Eden's toes clenched inside her satin slippers.

"When you visit Earth, you see it at its best. Your wishers are having their fantasies granted. They're

warm and happy. You don't see them when they're hurt-
ing each other. You don't see war or poverty or disease.
But those ugly, terrible things are part of the world too."

But to her, his words were meaningless. She knew
deep in her heart that Earth was beautiful and ripe with
the promise of adventure.

She whipped round to face him.

"What if it's worth all that to me? When did I ever
get to choose?"

A shadow of surprise flashed across Xavier's face.

"You didn't," he said. "And for that, you don't know
how lucky you are."

Six

Eden spent the rest of the evening in her room. She supposed Xavier and Goldie thought she was writing the report, but of course that wasn't true.

Her mind was racing as if powered by a steam engine. She couldn't stop wondering about the alumni she'd never heard from. If all the genies had been as grateful and well behaved as she'd been told, why didn't they communicate with the lamp?

Was it possible that Xavier and Goldie were lying? Maybe the other alumni *did* send messages. Maybe, for some reason, the lamp's masters just didn't want Eden to see them.

She kicked off her covers. If there were messages from the other alumni, they'd be filed in the drawers in the study. Surely she'd find answers in those drawers, if she could only explore them.

Of course, she wasn't allowed to enter the study alone. And yet, none of the lamp's doors had locks. Xavier said he didn't believe in them, which seemed strange, since he had no problem keeping her locked up in the lamp. So there had never been anything keeping her out of the study except the rule.

She thought about the report again. Maybe it was time to stop letting Xavier's rules hold her back.

Hours earlier, silence had filled the lamp like water in a glass. The last time the clocks had chimed, they'd struck two. It was safe to assume that Xavier and Goldie were long asleep.

Before she could lose her nerve, she sprang lithely from her bed.

Sneaking downstairs didn't prove to be difficult. The lamp's darkness cloaked her in secrecy and ushered her along. When she reached the study, she held her breath, gripped the gold doorknob, and gave it a push. When it opened obligingly, she slipped in and closed the door behind her. It was almost suspiciously simple.

She snapped her fingers to light a candle on Xavier's desk, then one on Goldie's. Together, the flames provided just enough light to give her her bearings.

Standing between the bookshelves that ascended higher than her eyes could see, she surveyed the room. It was her first time alone in the study. Dark and deserted, it seemed even larger than usual.

Her eyes combed the sky-high shelves, taking in rows upon rows of dusty volumes. Her gaze followed the ladders leaning against them from the floor to the top of the lamp. She examined Xavier's and Goldie's desks, and the empty leather chairs behind them. Between them, the silver telescope balanced gracefully on three slim legs.

Long before she'd started granting, she'd learned about the restrictions of the telescope's power. In Granting for Genies, she'd nearly combusted with excitement when Goldie had told her they could see all the way to Earth through the telescope. It was the best news she'd ever heard.

"I want to look!" she'd demanded. So Goldie had taken her down to the study. Hearing them, Xavier came out from the kitchen and joined them. Goldie lowered the telescope to her eye level. Ravenous for a view of the world she spent her days studying, she'd peered in expectantly.

But in an instant, her hopes fell like a popped balloon.

"It's not working!" she'd cried in dismay.

"Of course it's working," Goldie had said. "But the lamp is buried right now. There's nothing to see."

"That isn't fair!"

"Life isn't fair," Xavier had said matter-of-factly, and then Goldie led her back upstairs to finish lessons.

Since she couldn't go in the study alone, she'd never had a chance to try it again. But of course, it was safe to assume that if she hadn't been summoned, it was still buried. There'd be nothing to see.

But since she was here, why not try it anyway?

She moved to the delicate instrument and stood on her toes to reach the eye level where Xavier had left it. She couldn't risk them noticing it had been adjusted.

She leaned in, expecting nothing but darkness. But instead, she saw light—and heard voices.

Alarmed, she backed away.

She frowned. She hadn't been summoned. The lamp should be buried underground.

She placed her eye on the telescope again.

This time, she saw the backs of mortals sitting in rows of chairs. Men and women, dressed sharply in suits. There had to be hundreds of them. And at the front, a white-haired man in a suit and tie stood behind a podium and spoke to the crowd.

The telescope's powers enabled her to hear, as well as see, the scene. The man at the podium was speaking about global warming.

She stepped back again. It seemed that someone

sitting in the crowd, attending this event, was holding the lamp. Had this person found it but not yet rubbed it?

Suddenly, the study clock struck three. She nearly jumped out of her nightgown.

Time was limited—especially if the lamp was about to be rubbed. She needed to stay on task. She turned her attention to the drawers on the wall behind the desks.

Each drawer was as large as an oven you could cook a turkey in. She tiptoed to them, selected one randomly, and tugged its handle. It sprang toward her on tracks so slippery they might have been coated with grease, and crashed to the ground. She closed her eyes and bit her lip, hoping against all hope that her masters hadn't heard from their bedroom upstairs.

She rushed to replace the heavy drawer, but the grooves on the bottom wouldn't fit on the tracks properly. Blowing a stray piece of hair out of her face, she knelt in front of it.

She was so focused on fitting the drawer back in that she almost didn't notice the patch of gold wall showing through the space it had occupied. Across it was a curved silver bar that stretched about a foot wide.

Eden set the drawer gently on the floor and leaned forward to peer through the hole. Above the silver bar was another silver bar, and above that a third. She twisted her neck to look upward. The silver bars continued as far as she could see, one above another. She squinted, trying to make out how high they ascended. At a certain point, at least a story above, it looked like the wall curved outward at a pronounced angle.

She sank back on her heels. No other part of the lamp had a ladder built into the wall, and nowhere else did the wall curve so dramatically. What was back there, hidden behind the drawers?

She gripped the handle of the drawer above. This time she pulled it with just enough force so that it rolled gently from its tracks into her arms. Cradling it like it was made of porcelain, she set it on the floor with only the slightest hint of sound.

Next she removed the drawer below. The cavity she'd created was large enough to squeeze through.

Her arms, head, hips, and legs slipped through the opening, and her feet and hands found silver bars to cling to. With her elbows and knees out wide and her body pressed close to the wall, she scaled the slender ladder rungs. Considering that most days she couldn't make it across the kitchen without creating a mess, she had to marvel at how smoothly things were going. But she kept her focus on what was ahead—or, rather, above. She couldn't see what was coming, so she trusted her hands to find each new rung.

About twenty rungs up, she reached the point where

the wall curved sharply outward. Three rungs later, the ladder ended. The wall had curved to a nearly horizontal plane. Gripping the gold surface with her fingertips, she crawled forward.

As she slithered ahead, she realized the space she was crawling through was gradually decreasing in diameter. Like an electric shock it struck her: *she was inside the spout of the lamp.* As many times as she'd seen her home from the outside during grantings, she'd never stopped to wonder why no part of the lamp's interior resembled the spout. Her heart started racing. At the end of the spout was a *hole.* That meant an *opening to the world.*

With new zeal she crawled faster. The circumference of the space shrank until it cradled her like a cocoon. At last she found herself face-to-face with the lamp's only opening.

She stared at it in disbelief, heart pounding like a racehorse's hooves. The hole at the end of the spout was about the size of her outstretched hand. Through it was thick, murky darkness.

Suddenly a *whoosh* of wind flew forcefully in her face. Closing her eyes, she pulled back. What was happening?

She opened her eyes, and there he was—crouching right before her in the spout, directly in front of the open hole. Even in the dark, there was no mistaking his face.

She gasped. "Where did you come from?"

"Eden." Xavier's voice was sharp and urgent. He was just as shocked as she was.

"Where *were* you?" she cried. Her voice shook when she spoke. She realized her hands were trembling, too.

He took a deep breath. "Eden, I'll explain. Let's go back down—"

"Explain *now*!" She felt like a bubble in her chest had popped and was filling her lungs with hot liquid. "Did you just come into the lamp through that hole?"

He was wearing a suit like the men in the room she'd seen.

"You were just on Earth, weren't you? In that conference I saw through the telescope."

He paused. "I was attending the UN Climate Summit in New York City."

He'd been sitting there amongst them. On Earth. In New York City. The thought was too absurd to comprehend.

"But—*how*? Is that where the lamp will be found next?"

"No. By now, it could be anywhere on Earth."

"Is that hole the way out of the lamp?"

"It is," he said carefully. "Now, will you come with me?" He took her hand and edged around her. "Follow me down the ladder, and then we can talk."

Her mind buzzed like a swarm of honeybees. As

he guided her toward the ladder, she tried to pin down thoughts, but they flew away too quickly.

"Why didn't you *tell* me?" she demanded. She pulled her hand away from his. *"Why wouldn't you tell me?"*

He rubbed his face with his hand.

Eden felt heat on her cheeks and realized she was crying. "Do you just come and go as you please? How often do you go there?"

He swallowed. "I only leave because I have to. I *have* to bring back knowledge in order to keep your lessons current and relevant. New developments in technology, art, science. Can you imagine what would happen if we didn't have new information? For thousands of years? We'd be obsolete."

"But why don't you bring me *with* you?" she cried. "When you know I want to go?"

"Only one of us can leave the lamp at once," he said gently. "It won't allow more than that."

"You *lied* to me!" Every ounce of her body hummed with the sting of his betrayal.

"It wouldn't be right for you to go. You're not meant to roam among them."

"But *you* do it!"

"Only because I have to!" Xavier's eyes implored her. "If I could, I'd spend every minute in here with you and Goldie. Eden, the world is a dangerous place. Not to say it doesn't have its merits—it does. But there's also cruelty, death, pain. Things the lamp protects us from." His voice dropped. "Things I don't want you to see."

His words were no good to her. He didn't understand she wanted more than paradise.

"You're from a long, sacred line of genies," he went on. "Each one of you is graceful, brilliant, and terribly beautiful. You only grace mortals with your presence when you're granting. You *brighten* that cruel world when you're there."

"Well, you know what?" she said. "The world's not getting brightened by me anymore."

Xavier's eyebrows jumped to attention.

"I'm sick of living by these stupid rules," she said. "I'm *sick* of being something I never wanted to be."

"Don't—"

Her voice rose over his. "I'm *not* writing that stupid report, and I'm *not* granting any more wishes."

"Eden," he said firmly, "come with me. We'll sit down and talk about this." He tried to take her hand again, but it was too late for that.

"I quit!" she declared.

Fires lit in his eyes. "You can't quit! Young lady, you come with me right now!"

"Watch me!" Moving fast, Eden turned, pushed her body into the tight cocoon, and dove headfirst into the darkness. Somehow the small hole swallowed her up, and in an instant that delicious sensation of shuttling at supersonic speed was upon her and inside her. She heard Xavier's yell echoing behind her as if through a long tunnel, but before he could stop her she was out of the lamp.

Seven

Earth welcomed Eden with a kick in the head. Her first sensation was the impact of a bare foot straight between her eyes.

"What in the—what?" she heard a female voice say.

She opened her eyes, then immediately snapped them shut. The sunlight was excruciating for her lamp-sheltered vision.

She blinked, and gritty particles fell from her lashes. She shook her head, and more fell free. They covered her face; she even spat some from her mouth. But when she tried to lift her hands to wipe them off, she found they were stuck in place by her sides.

Of course, she thought. She'd climbed out of the spout before a mortal had discovered the lamp. Since it had been submerged underground, so, now, was she. Her body was totally buried, with only her head exposed. Her chin hadn't even cleared the surface.

Squinting, she could make out a girl squatting in front of her. She looked to be around Eden's age. She had shoulder-length brown hair with thick bangs, and she wore black sunglasses.

"Sorry I kicked you in the head," the girl said. "I mean, I guess. You can't really blame me. Your hair's the same color as the sand."

Sand. That must be what was all over her face. At least, with any luck, it would be less dense than dirt. She began to wriggle her hands toward the surface.

"What are you doing, anyway?"

Dazedly, Eden sized up her surroundings. All around her was sand, and above her—ahh. A clear blue sky, with not a trace of a cloud. She was on Earth, that much was certain. But where?

"Where am I?" she asked weakly.

The girl frowned. "Mission Beach?"

A beach! A thrill ran through her, all the way to her deep-buried toes.

She'd been on a beach once before. On a granting in Jamaica, she'd been summoned by a grizzled old man missing all of his hair and most of his teeth. He'd been using a metal detector to hunt for treasure along a secluded stretch of the coast. She'd been instantly infatuated with the grit of sand beneath her feet's tender soles and the sound of the ocean's waves crashing.

But the man had rattled off his wishes matter-of-factly,

with rip-roaring speed. You'd have thought he'd been expecting a genie for years and she'd showed up late for the appointment. She'd been sucked back into the lamp almost before she could memorize the sea's salty scent. There was no way to know when they might meet again.

But here it was: their second encounter. Now that she knew, she recognized the ocean's smell and gentle roar.

But where on Earth was Mission Beach? She racked her brain.

As if she'd heard Eden's unasked question, the girl added, "In San Diego?"

And then it clicked. "California?"

"Last time I checked." The girl laughed.

By now, almost all of Eden had surfaced. Her eyes, acclimated at last, opened fully. Suddenly her joy was uncontainable. What a lucky place to land!

"The *ocean*!" she squealed. The sparkling water rolled with waves. She kicked her feet madly to free her legs. Shielding her eyes, she turned her face skyward. High above, with no ceiling in sight, it was unthinkably, beautifully blue. And nestled grandly in the middle of the sky was that big, gorgeous sun.

"The *sun*!" Frantically she brushed sand off her shoulders, arms, and sides. "The *beach*!"

She jumped to her feet and turned in a circle ecstatically. Now that her vision was clear, she could see mortals strolling and lounging on brightly colored towels all over it. What a sight!

They were young and old, petite and enormous, curvy and slim, with a whole range of skin tones and a thousand different colors of hair. Skimpy swimwear exposed the intimate details of their bodies. Eden saw smooth-skinned, round-bellied, tottering toddlers. She saw long-legged women in bikini tops and old men with oversize ears and folds of skin hanging over their waistbands. She was awestruck by the countless ways they were put together.

Opposite the ocean and past the beach was a boardwalk where mortals moved in a brisk, happy summer rhythm. Rollerbladers and bikers zipped along one side, while mortals in swimwear cruised down the middle on foot.

Beyond the boardwalk loomed a number of strange structures, stretching high into the sky. She peered at them curiously. The most prominent was an apparatus built of wooden posts topped by a long, sloping track. The track rose high and dipped low, and little cars with no tops climbed to its heights and dropped to its depths. When she squinted, she could see groups of mortals sitting in the little cars. And when she strained, she could hear them screaming as the cars zipped around the track.

She recognized the apparatus. Xavier had briefed her on it during a unit on mortals' more puzzling leisure activities. If she remembered correctly, it was called a roller coaster.

Just then, a tiny creature covered in whitish fur ran up and sniffed at her feet. A bichon frise, Eden realized with glee.

A woman ran after it. "Sorry!" she said, smiling. "He's a little overly friendly."

"That's okay!" Eden said. "Can I pet him?" The woman nodded. Eden ran her hand over the dog's wavy fur, feeling the delicate bones beneath its skin. It panted and beamed at her. Eden was smitten.

After a moment the dog lost interest and ran on, with the woman chasing after. As she watched where they went, Eden's eye caught on a man with hair unlike any she'd ever seen. It was aqua blue, and it stood erect in a thin straight line that traveled from the middle of his forehead to the nape of his neck. She was stunned. He was carrying art on top of his head! She had to know how it was done. She raced to where he was spreading his towel.

"Excuse me!" she said. "How do you make your hair?"

He cast dull, darkened eyes on her. "How do I *make* it?" he repeated.

"It's lovely," she said. "Like a sculpture."

For some reason he seemed annoyed. "Haven't you ever seen a 'hawk?"

"A *hawk*," she said to herself. What a strange name for a hairstyle!

He raised his eyebrows. "Let me ask *you* something. Who wears a nightgown to the beach?"

Eden looked down at her ruffly white nightgown. She supposed it wasn't normal beach attire. And with good reason—it was *hot*. The sun was beaming down like it had a point to prove. She wiped sweat from her forehead. She could feel rivers of it trailing down her sides and a patch of it spreading on her back.

She squinted up at the boardwalk. Behind it was a row of shops. Shops sold clothes. She took off running through the sand toward it. Reaching the boardwalk, she weaved through throngs of beachcombers.

She ducked into a shop where mannequins in the window wore tank tops, shorts, and swimsuits in a rainbow of fluorescent hues. She paused for a moment to bask in the glory of the air-conditioning. She wasn't used to being hot or cold; in the lamp, the temperature was always just right.

Perusing the store's selection of weather-appropriate clothing, she tried to remember what she'd learned about buying things. Amongst all his needless facts and admonitions, it was the sort of practical information Xavier had never covered.

She examined a white tank top with the word *California* scrawled in hot pink across the front. She fingered the lightweight cotton longingly, then found the price tag tucked inside: $14.99. Fourteen dollars and ninety-nine cents. She'd never used money, and she certainly didn't own any. How did one go about getting it, anyway?

Feeling defeated, she weaved down the boardwalk again. Many of the people she saw were surfers. They were all different ages and types, but each carried a board like it was precious cargo, and kept his or her eyes fixed on the waves forming at the horizon. Watching them, she nearly ran into an athletic-looking, deeply tanned girl moving quickly across her path.

"You know I don't eat this crap!" the girl snapped at a young man following closely behind her. She was holding a white paper bag as far as possible from her body between two fingertips, as if it were a rancid dead rat. Reaching a trash can, she flicked it inside and strutted away with the male mortal hot on her heels.

A scruffy man in a tattered T-shirt appeared and sprang into action. He approached the can, retrieved the bag, and ripped out its contents: a cheeseburger wrapped in grease-soaked yellow paper and a cardboard box of French fries. He devoured it right there next to the garbage, then let out a satisfied puff of air, balled up the bag, and dropped it back in. He noticed Eden watching.

"Got a problem?" he snarled.

Baffled, she took a step back. This man needed a genie badly.

"Someone should teach you some manners," he said. With a shake of his head, he hobbled down the boardwalk.

She watched him go with mingled bewilderment and disgust. He'd eaten food out of the garbage! She hadn't known mortals could stoop so low.

But then an uneasy thought crossed her mind: the man wouldn't have taken that food unless he had nothing else to eat. What would prevent *her* from finding herself in the same position? Where would she find her next meal? This time tomorrow, would she be as desperate as he was?

Contemplating that, she faced the ocean and leaned on the rail. As she gazed at the glimmering water in the distance, a brilliant idea struck her: why not take a dip in the ocean? It would cool her off, *and* it was one of the things Xavier had forbidden. That alone was reason enough to try it.

In fact, she decided, she was going to do every last

thing he'd told her not to. And wasn't this a good place to start?

Inhaling the gorgeous ocean scent, she felt her adrenaline rising. For the first time, she was going *into the water*! She took off running, zigzagging around the towels that accented the sand like throw pillows.

When she reached the threshold, she paused to savor the sweet suspense. A wave rolled up and splashed her feet, and she gasped at the frigid temperature.

From her right came a shriek of delight. Someone nearby was having fun! She turned and spotted a man and a woman laughing and splashing each other. She jogged through knee-deep water to them and enthusiastically joined in. But as soon as she did, they stopped abruptly. Giving each other an odd look, they joined hands and walked toward the beach.

Why had they ended their fun? Eden shrugged and waded out further. She watched her pale feet through the clear, shallow water. She crouched down to let it wash over her whole body.

She looked out into the distance. The ocean went on forever! Of course she knew the Pacific was enormous — with an area of 63.8 million square miles, it covered one-third of Earth's total surface area. But memorizing those figures and seeing it stretch across the living room's big marble globe were nothing like beholding it in person.

She lowered her face to the surface and opened her lips to taste the chilled, salty water. How could Xavier call the lamp paradise after being exposed to this? Well, maybe he'd never have to leave his paradise again. Wasn't that what he wanted anyway? As long as she was on Earth, he was trapped in the lamp. Despite all his other lies, he must have told the truth about that. Otherwise, she was sure he would already have climbed out of the sand after her.

She'd left the lamp buried where she'd surfaced, which meant she was farther away from it than ever before. Xavier would lose his mind if he knew. The thought gave her a spark of satisfaction. Anyway, if a mortal happened to find it, she didn't think they'd be able to summon her, since she was already out in the world. And it wasn't like she was going to make a request for reentry.

As her mind wandered she waded deeper into the sea—so deep that before she knew it, she was standing on her tiptoes to keep her nose above water. The waves were coming more rapidly now, and the tug of the tide was stronger than she'd expected. Maybe, she thought uneasily, she *should* have learned to swim before venturing out this far.

It wasn't that she was frightened, but as the waves continued to assail her, she dearly wished for a moment to catch her breath.

Just as she'd resolved to retreat to shallower water, a wave crashed over her head. She emerged gasping for air and flapping her arms madly to stay afloat. Her feet could no longer find the ground. For the first time she understood the ocean's might, and she was afraid.

And then the big one hit.

Several things happened at once. Eden's mouth, throat, nose, and lungs filled with briny salt water that burned her eyes and nostrils with fiery fury. She was knocked back so roughly she lost all sense of direction, of orientation, of what was happening and where and why and how. She was spinning, twisting, upside down. Was that the ground scraping against her shoulder? She kicked madly and waved her arms desperately, hardly knowing for what she was reaching.

All she could be sure of, with the painful certainty of enlightenment come too late, was that Xavier had lied about one more thing. She wasn't really immortal. Because here, now, in the middle of the ocean, she was dying.

Of course, she didn't actually die. For one thing, she couldn't. But also, she was saved.

As she flailed and gasped, an arm encircled her waist and pulled her to the surface. The first gulp of air was like a knife to her chest, and the struggle didn't end as she was towed to shore through violent, unforgiving waves.

At last she and her savior reached dry land. He laid her flat on her back on the sand. Gagging, she coughed up a foul mouthful of water. Tears streamed from her eyes; her hands shook; her heart thumped painfully. Desperately she pushed up her sleeve and reached for her bracelet. When she felt its familiar shape, relief rushed over her.

Finally she staggered to her feet on legs as weak as a foal's. Before her was a crowd of gaping onlookers. As she gazed at them, they burst into cheers. With a jolt of shock, it hit her that they'd gathered to watch her rescue.

As her terror receded and the pain faded away, she became indignant. Attention was the last thing she needed. She turned to see who had dragged her into the limelight.

Somehow he looked familiar, though it was nearly impossible that they'd met before. He wasn't much older than Eden, but he stood several inches taller. He wore black swim trunks printed with a logo in green and blue. The sun had browned his skin to an even tan and sprinkled freckles across his face. His hair was dark and shaggy, with bangs that he tossed to the side with a whip of his head.

"Are you okay?" he asked.

"I'm ... fine," she said, her irritation fading. The observers were starting to disperse, but one of them came forward to stand beside him. It was the girl who'd kicked her in the head—the first mortal she'd seen.

"Are you sure?" the girl asked. She set her sunglasses on top of her head. "You were under for a really long time." She turned to the boy. "The lifeguards at this beach are worthless." And at once Eden realized why he looked so familiar: the two of them were nearly identical. The boy was slightly taller, but their swimmers' bodies, tan skin, freckles, and shiny straight chestnut hair were the same.

"You're twins!" she said.

The boy laughed. "Not quite. I'm a year older."

"But people think that all the time," the girl said.

The boy stuck out his hand. "I'm Tyler Rockwell. And this is my sister, Sasha."

It took Eden a moment to remember that handshakes were standard etiquette for American mortals when they met one another. She'd learned about them, but hadn't had an occasion to perform one. She reached out and took the hand in her own, then gave it a good firm shake. She was pretty sure that was how it was meant to go.

"I'm Eden," she said.

"Like the garden." Tyler smiled.

"Is that where you're from? The beginning of time?" Sasha smirked. "I mean, you're obviously not from around here. First you're buried in the sand, then you're drowning in the ocean."

"I just arrived," said Eden breathlessly.

"No kidding. You didn't exactly dress for the weather, did you?"

She looked down at her nightgown, now heavy with ocean water and hanging off her frame.

"Where are you from?" Tyler asked.

Eden frowned, wondering how to answer. "Sweden," she said at last.

"Eden from Sweden," Sasha said. "O-*kay*. Is this normal beach attire there?"

Tyler smacked her thigh with the back of his hand. *"What?"* she said. "I mean, come *on*!"

"Did the airline lose your luggage?" Tyler asked. "I've heard that happens all the time."

"Yeah," Eden agreed gratefully. "Can you believe it?"

Tyler eyed his sister. "Sasha," he said, "don't you always bring an extra swimsuit?"

Sasha looked at him disbelievingly. "Tyler! We don't even *know* her."

He raised his eyebrows at her. Eden's heart raced at the thought of changing out of her nightgown.

"Fine!" Sasha rolled her eyes and started digging in the tropical-print beach bag on her shoulder. She came up with a fistful of blue fabric and pushed it toward Eden.

"Thank you," Eden breathed. She'd never meant the words more.

Changing in the cramped stall of the beach restroom would have been difficult even if Eden knew how to put on a bikini, but she'd never had a reason to wear one before. Eventually she figured out which piece of flimsy fabric went where and which strings to tie in order to hold it all together.

"So. Have you moved here, or are you visiting?" Sasha asked from the other side of the bathroom stall's door.

Eden blinked. She was going to have to develop her alibi. For now, best to keep things vague. "I'll be here for a while," she said.

"Where are your parents? You didn't come here by yourself, did you?"

Eden stepped out of the stall and gasped at her reflection in the dim, smudged mirror. Instinctively she covered her chest and exposed stomach with her hands. She was nearly naked! She'd never worn so little clothing outside her bedroom before.

"What's wrong?" Sasha asked. "Looks like it fits."

This was what mortals did, Eden reminded herself. She was living like them now.

"If you want, you can put this on over." Sasha handed her a sheer cotton dress that was really just a long tank top. Eden felt much more comfortable with it on.

"Um..." Sasha was looking doubtfully at the wet nightgown balled up in Eden's hand. "Do you want to lay that out to dry?"

"Are you kidding? No." Eden tossed it into the garbage can. No matter what came to pass, she could never wear it again. "Worst outfit choice of my life."

Sasha laughed. "Ever since you climbed out of the

sand, I've been wondering what in the world you were thinking when you got dressed this morning."

"Trust me, you wouldn't believe me if I told you."

Tyler was waiting just outside the restrooms, with two surfboards leaning against the wall next to him. Another boy was with him. He was husky, with curly red hair and mischief in his eyes. "There you are!" Tyler said, grinning at Sasha. "We're starving. Let's go get burritos!"

"You're leaving?" Eden asked Sasha.

"Yeah, we still haven't had lunch."

The redheaded boy looked at Eden. "*Dude*. You're the girl who almost drowned? That was gnarly."

"I can get this stuff back from you some other time," Sasha said. She pulled out a slim black device and touched some of the images displayed on the screen, then handed it over. "Put in your number." Eden was mystified for a moment, but then she realized: *a cell phone*. She'd learned about them in the lamp—and even seen a few on grantings—but there had never been an opportunity to use one. She stared at it dazedly.

"Um, I don't—"

"Oh! Your Swedish phone probably doesn't work here, right? Unless you have international roaming."

"I—"

"Hello," said a beautiful woman who seemed to have

materialized right in front of her. Her dark brown hair was slicked into a low ponytail, and huge sunglasses covered her eyes. She wore a navy-blue polka-dot swimsuit.

"I saw your rescue from the ocean. It's lucky that this young man is such a good swimmer," she said, nodding toward Tyler.

He eyed her skeptically.

"I couldn't help but notice that gorgeous bracelet you're wearing," the woman said. "Can I see it?"

Eden's heart drummed with suspicion.

"Please?" the woman asked. "Just a look."

Slowly Eden held out her wrist in front of her. Quick as lightning, the woman pulled out a cell phone and pressed a button that made an electronic click.

Had she taken a photo? Eden jerked her wrist away.

"That looks like a very special bracelet. Where did you get it?"

Eden squinted at the woman. Did something about her look familiar? But that was impossible. She didn't know anyone on Earth.

"It's a family heirloom."

"Fascinating." The woman adjusted her sunglasses. "I wonder if I could take you for a bite to eat. We can chat about that bracelet, and other things."

"Actually, she's coming with us," Tyler interjected.

"Right?" He widened his eyes at Eden. "Want to come have a burrito?"

Her heart nearly leaped out of her chest. "I *love* burritos!"

"They have burritos in Sweden?" Sasha asked doubtfully.

The woman seemed perturbed. "Maybe we'll see each other again," she said, though Eden couldn't imagine why they would. "What was your name?"

"Eden."

"Eden." The woman broke into a smile, showing perfect white teeth. "I do hope we'll meet again."

"What was *that* all about?" Sasha asked as they walked away.

Eden shrugged, trying to forget the weird interaction. She was glad to leave the woman behind. But she couldn't shake the nagging feeling that she'd seen her before—or the suspicion that she'd see her again.

Violet's phone buzzed. Her boss hadn't stopped texting since she'd sent her the photo of the girl who'd been rescued from the ocean: the girl whose face she and her colleagues had memorized nearly two years earlier. They'd gotten the image from a stolen parchment-paper message.

Now that she'd captured a close-up of the bracelet,

there was no question. That bracelet could only mean one thing.

This time it was a call. Sighing, Violet answered.

"What's happening?" demanded the voice on the other end.

"They're walking to a burrito shack down the road. I'm following."

"You couldn't get her away?"

"She wouldn't come."

"Is she still with the boy who saved her?"

"Yes, and another boy, and a girl. His sister, I think."

"Violet, you don't have long. Whichever of those kids is her wisher will make those wishes faster than you can say 'paradise.'"

"I *know*. I'm doing the best I can."

Her boss was silent. Violet could picture her in the back of her black limo, speeding through Paris to the airport where her private jet would be waiting. She'd be white-knuckled, stilettos tapping like mad. Thinking of a way to get what they all wanted, obsessed over, lived for.

"You still haven't seen the lamp?"

"No."

"You've got to find out where it is. It can't be far."

"I know."

"And you've got to get her away from those mortals."

Violet glanced at the row of kids walking fifty feet ahead. "I know."

"He could make those wishes at any moment. And once he does, the lamp will be out of our reach again. In a new randomly selected spot, anywhere on Earth."

"I *know*. I know how the lamp works as well as you do. Remember?"

"Right." Violet's boss took a deep breath. "Violet, I trust you."

"Thank you."

"Don't mess up." The line went dead.

Violet rolled her eyes. Her boss was such a micromanager. But Violet knew she was excited, too. It was a huge coup that she'd spotted the girl: Electra's first genie sighting in over fifty years. And where the genie was, the lamp couldn't be far.

Naturally, it had happened when Violet was supposed to be on vacation. As if that really existed for the women who were part of Electra—or, as they'd come to be known, the Electric. Their work was their passion and their purpose. It had been that way for centuries. Violet's boss, the founder, was a woman whose devotion to the cause was unsurpassed.

After all, this was no normal business. The Electric had committed their lives to acquiring the lamp.

Violet rubbed the place on her right wrist where

she used to wear her own genie bracelet. She'd taken it off centuries ago. Her boss forbade them, teaching that they signified the tyranny they'd all lived under at one point. Removing the bracelet showed you were free.

Up ahead, she watched the brother and sister lean their surfboards against the stucco exterior of a Mexican restaurant; then the four kids went inside. Violet sat at a discreet table outside the café next door.

She had a good feeling about this. At last, here was a chance to prove her worth—to her boss, and to the others. She wouldn't let it pass her by.

Nine

There was no way the mortals could have imagined the momentousness of lunch at Manny's Mexican Cocina. Xavier and Goldie were the only people Eden had ever eaten a meal with. Come to think of it, she'd never had a real conversation with anyone else.

She was still shaken by what had happened in the ocean. On the one hand, she was annoyed with herself for panicking. Her predecessors had survived blazing fires and catastrophic car crashes because their duties were not yet complete. Drowning was impossible for her. Still, for the first time she'd glimpsed what it was *like* to be mortal, and the terror of it was astonishing. How could mortals bear to face each day with death as a constant threat?

But there was no point dwelling on that. She was on Earth, feasting on Mexican food with mortals. She was *free*. And so far, freedom was delicious.

"This is *great!*" she said. She beamed at the faces around her and took another giant bite. Including Eden, seven of them sat around the blue-tiled table—Tyler, Sasha, the redheaded boy, and three other friends who'd met them there. She'd never seen so many young people at once. And the best part was, they all thought she was a mortal like them.

Chewing happily, she soaked in the restaurant's atmosphere. Though she'd never been to Mexico, she gathered that the décor, like the food, was of Mexican influence. The walls were yellow, with brightly colored tiles outlining the doorways and sombreros tacked up here and there. Lively music Eden recognized from music lessons as mariachi rolled jovially from the speakers and through the air.

"So you're from Sweden?" the boy with red hair asked. He'd introduced himself as Devin.

The other boy, Cameron, was contagiously good-natured. His friendly face was framed by shoulder-length jet-black hair. "Isn't it, like, way cold there?" he asked.

Luckily Xavier had just finished a unit on Sweden. It was probably why she'd used it as her alibi. "The north is really cold," she said, "but the south, where I'm from, is temperate. Winter temperatures generally range from minus four to two degrees Celsius, or"—she thought fast—"twenty-five to thirty-six degrees

Fahrenheit. In the summer, temperatures rise to around sixty-eight to seventy-seven degrees Fahrenheit. Not cold, but definitely not as hot as it is here." She smiled and sipped her water.

The faces around the table went as blank as erased blackboards. Tension hung in the air like a bad smell. She sensed she'd misspoken, but she wasn't sure how.

"Is something wrong with this sauce?" she asked, to break the silence. "It's supposed to be extra spicy, but I can't taste a thing."

"Dude," Devin said in awe, "this is the hottest sauce north of the border. What do they *feed* you over there?"

Eden felt her cheeks flush. Thanks a lot, Xavier, she thought. She pushed up her sleeves and fanned her face.

One of the girls at the table squinted at Eden. Her name was Skye, and her hair was frosted silvery blond. "Who are you again, and why are you here?"

"She almost drowned!" Devin said. "Tyler rescued her." He scraped the last bit of guacamole from a bowl in the middle of the table onto a tortilla chip.

"Tyler *rescued* her?" Skye looked at him disbelievingly. "Isn't that the lifeguards' job?"

"The lifeguards were totally MIA," Sasha said. "Seriously, if it wasn't for him, she would have died."

Not exactly, Eden thought—but they didn't need to know that.

"Why don't you know how to *swim*?" asked the other

girl, Claire. When she started talking, Eden had to hide her surprise at the metal mechanism in her mouth. A square post was affixed to the middle of each tooth, and the posts were connected by thin silver wires. Eden was mystified. Was this something mortals wore for decoration, like makeup or jewelry?

"Can you let up?" Tyler said. "She's visiting from Sweden."

"Oh yeah? For how long?" Skye shot the words at her viciously.

"If you're foreign, then where's your accent?" Claire asked, narrowing her eyes.

Eden jammed the very large remaining portion of her burrito in her mouth and held up a finger to buy time.

Fortunately, just then, a waiter cleared the plates and glasses and set a white slip of paper on the table. Skye picked it up and examined it. "Eight bucks each," she announced. Everyone reached below the table to fumble in their pockets.

For a moment Eden didn't know what was going on. Then it hit her: they had to *pay* for the food!

"Tyler, you owe me," Sasha said.

"Yeah, yeah, I've got it," Tyler sighed, plunking a few bills on the table. He turned to Eden. "Have you gotten your currency exchanged yet?"

Again Eden was lost for words. "I don't . . ."

He squinted at her curiously. "I'll get yours," he said. "You can pay me back." He fished another bill out of his battered brown leather wallet and added it to the pile. Eden felt giddy with gratitude.

"Let's go back to the beach," Sasha said. "Starting tomorrow, I'll have no more free afternoons—not with volleyball *and* babysitting."

They all started sliding out of the booth.

"I've got to bounce," Cameron said.

"Claire and I are going back-to-school shopping," said Skye as the group spilled out the door. She batted her mascara-thickened lashes. "Tyler, do you want to come?"

"When I can surf? Are you joking?" he said, pulling his board off the wall outside. The girl's face deflated like a popped balloon.

"Girl, I'll go to the mall with you!" Devin said, draping his arm around her.

She rolled her eyes. "That's okay," she said, ducking away and linking arms with Claire.

Eden was observing all of this so absorbedly, she almost didn't notice Tyler watching her. Her eyes darted away when they made contact with his, but when she looked back he smiled.

Maybe her drowning scare hadn't been such a bad thing after all.

Back at the beach, Eden trailed Tyler and Sasha as they searched for the perfect spot, carrying their surfboards under their arms. As they did, she noticed a sand castle rising from the ground. A chubby little girl with dark pigtails shaped towers and turrets as tall as she was with clumsy hands and colorful toys. Eden's breath caught in her throat when she spotted a gold oil lamp propped between two of the turrets.

Her lamp.

With a start, she realized the sand castle was right near where she had surfaced. *Exactly where the lamp was buried.* And in the ground next to it was a deep, wide hole.

"You guys go ahead," she said. "I'll find you later."

Sasha shrugged.

"We'll be just over here, to the right a little further," said Tyler. She nodded, and they moved along.

With her eyes on the lamp, Eden moved toward the sand castle. She was just about to pluck it free when a red plastic shovel slapped her hand away.

"MY genie lamp!!" the pigtailed girl screeched, wielding her tiny weapon.

Just then, an extremely large man walked up, dropped the buckets of wet sand he'd just carried from the ocean, and positioned himself menacingly between Eden and the sand castle. Dark illustrations were inked all over his biceps and beefy chest. The most prominent one stretched in a curve under his neck: thick Gothic letters that spelled the word *Romeo*.

"Why you trying to steal a toy from a kid?" the man growled.

"Actually it's *mine*," Eden said. She tried to reach around him, but his massive arm blocked her. He took the lamp in his bulky fingers, and Eden's eyes widened— even they were imprinted with letters.

The girl wrapped her arms around his leg. "Why you telling lies to a nice little girl?" One of his front teeth gleamed shiny gold in the sun.

"It's not a lie!" Eden cried. "I swear it's mine!"

He shook his head matter-of-factly. "Me and my daughter dug it up out of the sand ourselves."

"We're gonna finish this castle, and then we're gonna rub it and a genie's gonna come grant my wishes," the girl said in a singsongy voice.

"But there's no genie in there!" Eden protested.

The girl's face crumpled up in indignation. "YES THERE IS!" she insisted.

"No, there's not!" Eden said. "It's just a worthless lamp. Look, it's not even shiny." Now that she looked at it, the lamp *did* look pretty dinky from the outside.

It was so dull and scuffed up, you wouldn't even know it was made of solid gold. It was hard to believe the world where she'd grown up was inside.

The man puffed out his chest and pushed back his shoulders. "Hey," he said. "Why don't you leave my little angel alone and get out of here?"

But the girl was determined to prove Eden wrong. "I'll show you!" she said, her chubby cheeks reddening. She pulled the lamp from Romeo's grip.

Eden was suddenly apprehensive. What if she'd been wrong? What if she *could* still be summoned even though she was on Earth, and this little monster was about to become her next wisher? "Wait—" she yelled, but the girl was already rubbing like mad.

And rubbing, and rubbing, and rubbing. Eden held her breath and the man looked on with mild interest, but nothing happened.

Eden let out a sigh of relief. She couldn't be summoned. And the girl would never guess Eden was the genie she wanted so badly. No one would. As long as she didn't tell anyone the truth, she could keep posing as a mortal and she'd never have to grant a single wish.

Furiously the girl stomped her foot in the sand. "It's not working!"

"See?" Eden said. "It's worthless. May as well give it back to me."

But the girl shook her head defiantly. "No way!"

"If you want it so bad," the man with the Romeo tattoo said, "you got something to give us for it?"

"Like what?"

"Got any money?"

Money again. She *had* to figure out how to get some. But then Romeo's eyes dropped to Eden's wrist.

"That bracelet," he said, pointing. "Is it real?"

Eden's heart started pounding.

"Give me that bracelet," he said. His gold tooth showed when he smiled. "Then I'll give you the lamp."

There was absolutely no way she was giving up the bracelet. She'd ignore all Xavier's warnings except for that one.

But she couldn't lose the lamp either. How could she outsmart this mortal and keep both?

All at once, the strangest thing happened. For a split second the bracelet glowed brightly. Eden felt a pulse of power around her wrist, and a weight in her hand. She looked down and saw that, somehow, she was holding the lamp.

"What the heck?" Romeo said. "How'd you do that?"

The girl's face screwed up, and she started to wail. "She took it from me!"

Eying Eden warily, Romeo picked the girl up in his arms. "Let's play somewhere else, angel. Somethin' weird's going on."

Eden tightened her grip on the lamp and walked

quickly away. She was floored by what had just happened. Even though magic made her world go round, to see it used so fiercely for the protection of her and the lamp was sort of baffling—but also, comforting.

"What do you know! We meet again!" It was the dark-haired woman. As before, she'd popped up directly in Eden's path. "And you've got another treasure." The lamp had her practically drooling. "What a beauty that one is."

"Thanks. Look, I've got to meet my friends."

"Can I tell you why you've caught my interest?" The woman didn't wait for an answer. She whipped a small card out of her purse and handed it over.

V

ELECTRA

A FINE AUCTION HOUSE

+33 1 40 76 85 85

"I work for one of the world's top auction houses. That lamp and your bracelet are both items we'd be very interested in buying."

Eden looked at the card and shook her head. "They're not for sale."

"I don't think you understand. You can name your price."

Eden squinted at the woman again. She wished she could figure out why she recognized her. "Like I said," she said carefully, "I'm not going to sell the lamp, or the bracelet." She started walking forward, stepping around towels and sunbathers, searching for Sasha's tropical-print beach bag.

"You don't have to decide right now!" the woman said, staying alongside her. She was starting to sound desperate. "I can take you to dinner. We'll discuss your options."

"No," Eden said firmly. "Can you leave me alone now? Like I said, I'm going to meet my friends."

The woman was visibly distressed. "Well," she said, "keep the card. Think about it. You might change your mind."

"That's not going to happen." Eden wished she knew exactly where Tyler and Sasha were. She looked up toward the ocean and saw, between waves, flashes of a strange figure emerging. It was larger than a normal person, with extra limbs sticking this way and that. Seeing it, she was struck with a funny feeling.

Only when Tyler tossed his hair was she sure that it was them. He was crossing the remaining stretch of ocean on foot, and instead of his surfboard he was carrying Sasha. Eden ran to meet them.

Reaching dry land, Tyler set his sister down. Sasha's

face was contorted in pain, and tears were leaking from the corners of her eyes. Eden's gaze traveled from her distraught expression down her torso, to the end of her leg. There, at the bottom, was the problem: her ankle was swollen like a water balloon filled to bursting.

Eden's stomach curled. *What was wrong with that foot?*

Sasha let out a cry that seemed to rise from deep inside her chest. Eden couldn't stop staring. She'd never seen someone cry before, except when overexcited wishers shed tears of joy. She'd cried herself, of course, when Xavier was being particularly unfair or on long, lonely nights in the prison of her bedroom. But the echo of her wails through the lamp's empty caverns was different from these sobs.

She turned to Tyler. "What *happened*?"

"Bad sprain, I think." He cupped the bloated ankle in his hand delicately, like he was holding a baby chick. Cautiously he lifted it, prompting Sasha to release another miserable moan. He examined the elevated ankle, speaking to Eden without looking her way. "Hey, run and get a lifeguard. I can't believe how useless they are."

Lifeguard. The same word Sasha had mentioned after Tyler had saved her from the sea. For a horrible instant she recalled how she'd felt when the wave had held her under. Was that how Sasha felt now?

If Sasha needed someone to guard her life, her injury must be serious. Eden couldn't die, but Sasha certainly could.

"Eden," Tyler said. "Go get the lifeguard!"

"There's no way I can play volleyball now!" Sasha wailed.

Eden shuddered. She'd learned about mortals' injuries in Xavier's anatomy lessons, and now she wished she'd paid more attention. Was it possible to die from an ankle sprain? Panic had made a sticky mess of her mind.

"What's *wrong* with you?" The impatience in Tyler's voice rang out. "Get the lifeguard!"

Eden took a deep breath. She couldn't believe what she was about to do, but she also couldn't watch Sasha suffer for one more moment. "Tyler," she said firmly, "wish for Sasha's injury to go away."

Tyler twisted toward her, his face crinkling in confusion. *"What?"*

Glancing to the right, Eden saw a middle-aged woman approaching a guy in red board shorts standing about fifty yards away at the foot of a tall white stand. She tapped him on the shoulder and pointed toward Eden, Tyler, and Sasha. He yelled something to the red-suited girl sitting high in the seat above him and started jogging in their direction.

Eden took in the rest of the area. Other mortals had

noticed too. One was V, the dark-haired woman. She stood a short distance away, watching intently.

"*Wish* it," she urged. "Out loud." After the incident with Romeo and his daughter, it seemed crazy to offer a wish. She'd been petrified that she'd find herself locked into one granting, yet now here she was volunteering for another.

"What are you *talking* about?" Tyler yelled. "We need *help*."

Sasha let out a fresh sob. In her peripheral vision, Eden saw the mortal in red shorts approaching.

"*Listen* to me," she said, her voice rising. She spoke with more conviction than she felt, ignoring the doubts in the corner of her mind. All she could see was the agony on Sasha's face, and all she wanted was to erase it. "Repeat these words: I wish for Sasha's ankle to be healed."

Tyler gritted his teeth. "If I say it, will you help me?"

"Yes!" Eden said desperately.

"Fine!" he yelled. "I wish for Sasha's ankle to be healed!"

Without a word, Eden held out her hand and snapped.

It took a few moments for Sasha to realize she no longer felt any pain. She fell silent mid-sob. A dazed sense of quiet settled over them like soft snow falling from the sky.

"Sash?" Tyler began. "Did you . . ." He looked down

at the foot he was holding. The swelling had vanished; its size and shape were perfectly normal. He dropped it in the sand like it had gone scalding hot. Both of them stared in wonder while Sasha pointed and flexed it.

The relief that washed over Eden was so powerful it made her dizzy. And there was something else too: satisfaction. For the first time, she was proud of a wish she'd granted.

"I'm here!" the lifeguard announced importantly as he arrived.

"We don't need you," Eden said.

Confusion crossed the lifeguard's face. "That lady over there said a girl was hurt."

Eden saw Tyler and Sasha lock eyes and come to a wordless agreement. "She was wrong," Sasha sniffed. "Nothing happened."

"Are you sure?"

"She's *fine*," said Tyler. "She thought she'd cut her foot, but she imagined it."

The lifeguard stared at him uncertainly, then turned to Eden again. He blinked and shrugged. "All right," he said. "If you're sure."

"We're sure."

The lifeguard jogged back to the stand. Eden was relieved to be rid of him. But as his figure faded, reality set in: she'd just granted a wish. There would be consequences.

—

Frantically, Violet typed an update for her boss.

First, she reported that Eden now had the lamp—but refused to part with it, or even discuss it. She was a stubborn little thing.

If Violet had reached the beach before Eden, she might have been able to snag the lamp herself. But if the genie was still wearing the bracelet, it wouldn't do any good anyway. The lamp would always return to the genie unless the bracelet was removed.

Secondly, she reported that she'd seen the female mortal's foot instantaneously healed. So that was one wish. Violet's boss wouldn't be happy about that. Eden hadn't vanished, so it wasn't the third wish. However, time was ticking.

Violet's hands shook as she pressed the button to send the message. Within a minute, she had a reply:

> Looks like I'll have to handle this myself
> when I arrive.
> Don't lose the girl.
> Sylvana

Ten

"How'd you *do* that?" Tyler asked.

Eden couldn't believe how foolish she'd been. Five minutes ago she'd been free, with the whole world in front of her; now, she was bound to a wisher. Her time on Earth would end as soon as his third wish had been granted.

But just as she was about to launch into the rules, something stopped her. Tyler and Sasha had no idea that Eden had come from the lamp. They hadn't even seen it yet.

A thought occurred to her. What would happen if she didn't tell them at all?

"What's this?" Sasha swiped the lamp from Eden's lap, where she'd dropped it when she'd sat down.

"That's weird," Tyler said, taking it. He examined it closely. "You know what it looks like? A genie lamp. Like from those old stories."

Sasha took it back from him. She raised her eyebrows at Tyler. "Are you thinking what I'm thinking?"

Tyler laughed. "No way!"

"Hear me out!" Sasha's eyes were wide. "You *wished* that my ankle would be healed, and then it happened. Like *magic.*"

"Like a genie granted the wish?" Tyler shook his head. "That's completely nuts."

"But you *saw*!" Sasha insisted. "It was like I'd never hurt my ankle." Absently she squeezed the ankle, as if to ensure it was still unhurt. Her eyes lit on Eden. *"You!"*

Eden gritted her teeth.

"You're the one who told him to wish I was healed. Is that your lamp?"

Eden tried to think fast. "I . . . found it."

"Where? On the beach?"

"Yeah, just over there." She pointed toward the sand castles. "While you guys were surfing."

Tyler's eyes searched hers, and she tried her best not to look guilty. "How were you so sure that making a wish would work?"

Eden shrugged. "I wasn't. It was just a hunch."

Tyler was thinking hard, like he was replaying the scene in his mind.

Sasha looked perplexed too. "If you thought there was any chance this lamp could grant wishes, why would you want to give one up?" she asked. "You only just met us."

"It was important," Eden said. "I wasn't going to let you *die*."

The way they looked at her, you'd have thought she'd said she was going to fish her wet nightgown out of the trash and put it back on. They burst out laughing.

"Let me *die*?" Sasha said. "Let's not get overly dramatic. Don't get me wrong, sprained ankles hurt like hell. But it's not like it was going to *kill* me."

Eden felt like she'd missed an easy question on a test. Sasha hadn't been in mortal danger after all. What a waste.

"But you wanted a lifeguard..."

"Because I needed ice! Trust me, I've survived a few sprained ankles in my time. Haven't you?"

Eden tried to think of how to answer.

"Wait a second," Tyler said. "*If* this is a real genie lamp—and I'm still not convinced that it is—wouldn't that mean there's a genie who granted that wish?"

"Oh yeah," Sasha said. "Eden, did you see a genie?"

Eden paused. "No..." Technically, it was true.

"Okay. Let's say this *is* a genie lamp," Sasha said. "You're supposed to get three wishes, right? Do you think since we used one wish, now we get two more?"

Eden's skin prickled with fear. If Tyler were to make

a wish, she'd have no choice but to grant it. Though she was sort of able to decide *how* to grant a wish, she couldn't refuse to grant it unless the rules were violated. There was a delicate balance between the wisher's words, the genie's mind, and the will of the lamp. Eden wasn't even sure exactly how it worked. She could imagine the way a wish would be granted, but the lamp itself produced the results. In Granting for Genies, Goldie had described it this way: for a genie, granting was kind of like breathing. You can breathe through your mouth or your nose, take a deep or shallow breath, but you can't decide you're not going to breathe.

"Two more wishes," Tyler said thoughtfully. "If we're going to give this a shot, then we'd better make them good."

"We'll come up with the best wishes ever," Sasha said. "Like a mansion. With...a garage full of Range Rovers?"

Tyler rolled his eyes. "Lame."

"Well, I don't know! What do you want, Ty?"

"Be careful!" Eden interrupted. The longer she could delay their wishes, the better. "Since Tyler made the first wish, I *bet* that if he says he wishes for something, he won't be able to take it back."

She watched the logic sink in. "You're right," Tyler said. "We've got to be careful. We don't want to waste them."

"That's right! You should think about it for a while. Strategize." This was good. This could buy her more time—a few hours, at least.

"Sash, our boards have probably washed up onshore," Tyler said. "Want to go see?"

"Yeah. No way we can afford new ones."

"Well, at least not yet," Tyler said with a smile. "You'll wait here with the lamp?" he asked Eden.

"No problem."

As they went back toward the ocean, Eden let out a slow breath. What a close call! But she was still on Earth. Nothing else mattered.

With a start, she remembered something unsettling. No doubt Xavier and Goldie were watching through the telescope. They could probably see and hear everything that was happening.

She looked down at the lamp again. This time, a rolled-up piece of parchment squeezed through the spout and landed in her hands.

Across it, in tight neat script, were four words: *Eden of the Lamp.*

She glanced up to see Tyler and Sasha at the shoreline. They'd retrieved one board, but were still searching for the other. Eden took a deep breath and unrolled the parchment.

Xavier and Goldie's faces appeared, half-lit and wan in the dim study. Behind them were the familiar shelves of ancient books. The lamp's shadowy interior was a stark and unappealing contrast to the sun-brightened beach.

"Eden!" Xavier said urgently. "Listen to us! This is very important." Dark circles underlined his panicked eyes.

Goldie was no less disheveled. Wisps of hair had escaped her bun, and with a twinge of remorse, Eden realized her puffy face meant she'd been crying.

"We know you're angry. But you must listen. You're in serious danger out there—much more serious than you can imagine."

"We saw you recover the lamp from that tattooed mortal and his daughter." Goldie shuddered. "And we saw you grant a wish for that boy."

"But if you make a request for reentry, you won't have to grant his other two wishes! Please, come home," Xavier pleaded.

It was strange to see him like this. Nothing rattled him. But now he was helpless for the first time, and obviously he had no idea how to handle it.

Goldie turned and whispered something in his ear. Xavier tugged on his mustache. "There's something you need to know," he said. "Listen very carefully, Eden. There are people on Earth who are desperate to seize the lamp's power for their own evil purposes. And their only chance of doing that is through you."

"What are you doing?" Sasha was standing over Eden. In a rush, Eden crushed the parchment paper into a ball in her fist.

"Nothing," she said. "Just looking at this weird drawing I found."

"You sure do find a lot of things." Sasha adjusted the surfboard under her arm.

Eden stood up. "You got the boards?"

"Only Sasha's," said Tyler as he walked up. Sasha's beach bag was on his shoulder. "Someone must have taken mine." He shrugged. "I don't blame them—it was a good board."

"So, look. Are you going to tell us what you're doing here?" Sasha asked. "Because we really don't know anything about you, except that you just got here from Sweden."

Eden bit her lip.

"Did anyone come with you?" Tyler pressed. "Your parents?"

"My mom," Eden lied.

"Okay . . . where is she?"

"Well, she was supposed to come. But . . ." At that moment, an airplane flew across the sky, providing a fresh burst of inspiration. "Her flight was canceled."

"Why was she on a different flight than you?" Sasha seemed doubtful.

"She was coming from . . . Japan."

"Wow. International family. Okay."

"Yeah. So she should be here . . . tomorrow. I think."

"Right. So what are you doing until then?"

Eden looked between the two of them uneasily. "I'm not sure."

"And you don't have money, a cell phone, or a place to stay?"

She shook her head slowly. It wasn't a very plausible story.

Tyler seemed concerned. "That doesn't sound like a good situation. What does she expect you to do?"

"Where's your dad?" Sasha asked dubiously.

"Somewhere in Sweden. We haven't heard from him in years."

Tyler and Sasha exchanged a sympathetic look.

"And you don't know *anyone* in San Diego?" Sasha asked.

Eden shook her head again.

"Well, you know us now," Tyler said. "At this point, we're all in this together anyway. We've got to figure out what to do with this lamp." He shrugged at Sasha. "Why doesn't she stay with us tonight?"

Eden had to press her lips closed so she wouldn't let out a scream of excitement.

"I don't know, Ty," Sasha said uncertainly. "School starts tomorrow, remember?"

"I'm supposed to go to school too," Eden said, simply

because, as a mortal, it seemed like the most natural thing.

"Really? Are you moving to San Diego?"

"Yes." She was speaking faster than she could think things through. It felt sort of like tumbling down a hill.

"Well why didn't you say so before?" Tyler said. "You can stay the night and come to school with us, and then your mom will be here tomorrow and help you figure everything out. Right?"

"Right." At least it would give her time to come up with a new solution.

"Then that's settled. Why don't we keep the lamp in here?" Tyler held the bag open so Eden could drop it in, and together, the three of them started across the beach.

"Why are you still carrying that drawing?" Sasha asked. "Here's a trash can."

"Oh, great," Eden said. "I was just looking for one."

With a flash of remorse, she tossed the parchment paper still balled up in her hand into the trash. She'd been hoping they wouldn't notice it.

She supposed she'd never know what Xavier was going to say next. She could only hope it wasn't important.

Eleven

In Eden's experience, mortals were pretty darn predictable. She liked to play a little game within the first minute of being summoned where she guessed what a wisher would wish for. Usually she wasn't too far off.

Naturally, money was a big one. This took a variety of forms. Often mortals wished for the largest lump sum they could think of—a million dollars, a billion pounds, a trillion yen, etc. Several times she'd had to inform a wisher that a zillion or a bajillion was not a real or finite number, so she was unable to grant a wish for that amount. Some people (like Darryl Dolan of Wagga Wagga, Australia) wished to win the lottery. The truth was, most lottery jackpot winners on Earth only won because of a granted wish. But if the wisher didn't provide details regarding the win, the genie had the flexibility to have a bit of fun. And always, if possible, Eden liked to have fun.

Of course, mortals wished for other things too. Women wished for beauty, forgetting that beauty always fades. Men wished for beautiful wives, ignorant to the fact that those wives could leave them. Children wished for superpowers, only to find that society is not kind to those who are different. Most of them would spend the rest of their lives wishing they could be normal, but without a genie in sight to help them.

Some wishers asked for fame, not knowing that fame brings hatred more often than love. Many wanted intelligence, athletic prowess, or musical talent. These were the wishes that ended up in the course guide. But eventually those wishers learned that running a world-record mile or producing a number-one album doesn't guarantee happiness. Often it makes it more elusive.

Another common request was love. Eden couldn't think of anything more pathetic. There were over seven billion people on Earth. Anyone who couldn't find love on her or his own must be either socially incompetent or totally lazy.

Every now and then someone wished to help another person, but that was rare. In Eden's experience, those wishes weren't at the front of mortals' minds. A boy who'd summoned her in Latvia had wished for his wheelchair-bound grandfather to walk, and the woman in Usson had wished for a cure for her baby's colic.

But those were the only ones she'd encountered. Almost without fail, mortals' wishes were for themselves.

"Where should we start?" Sasha said. "Eden, what do you think?" They'd left the beach, gone down the boardwalk past the roller coaster, and were strolling down a quiet sidewalk.

"Think about what makes you happy," Eden said distractedly. Her first sunset was tinting the sky with soft shades of magic, and she couldn't tear her eyes away.

"Winning," Sasha said promptly. She kicked a stray soccer ball that had drifted their way from a nearby group of kids.

"The ocean," said Tyler.

"Getting good grades. Succeeding."

"Surfing. Listening to music."

"New shoes."

"New boards. Hey," Tyler said. "I never found my board. We could ask for a new one."

"We can't *just* ask for a new board," Sasha said. She shifted her bag to the other shoulder. "We can do *way* better than that."

"Are you guys seeing this sunset?" Eden said. "It's unbelievable."

Tyler and Sasha looked toward the horizon like they'd never noticed it before.

"Sure, I guess," Sasha said. "If you like that kind of thing."

"I've got an idea," Tyler said. "We could wish to travel."

"Yes," Sasha agreed.

"How's Sweden this time of year?"

"Here is *way* better than Sweden," Eden answered quickly.

"Really?" He shrugged. "It'd be cool to see it, anyway."

"Anywhere that's not here would be cool." Sasha sighed. "I need a new scene."

"We could go somewhere with amazing beaches. Like Hawaii, or Bali." Tyler grinned. "All I'd do is surf and lie on the sand. Nothing to worry about, nothing to get you down."

"Too secluded for me," Sasha said. "I'd want to go to a city. Somewhere like London, or Paris, or New York, where I could meet lots of interesting new people. Here, everyone's the same."

"Wait a second," Eden interrupted. "You live in America, but you've never been to New York?"

"We've never even left California," Tyler said.

"Why not?" This was the type of thing that frustrated her about mortals. Why did they take the world's wideness and greatness for granted?

"Can't afford it." Tyler smiled. Eden couldn't think of a response. Now that he'd mentioned it, she supposed you would need money for food and shelter while traveling. She was starting to understand why mortals were so quick to wish for it.

Abruptly, he stopped and turned around.

"What are you doing?" Sasha asked.

"I swear I keep hearing someone behind us, but every time I look there's no one there."

"Spooky," Sasha said sarcastically, rolling her eyes at Eden. "You know, we live in a free country. People are *allowed* to walk behind you."

"Yeah, yeah." Tyler rejoined them—but after a few steps he stopped again and held his hands out, palms to the sky. "You feel that?"

"What are you imagining now?" Sasha teased.

Tyler caught Eden's eye and smiled. "This time it's real." His teeth were a little bit crooked, like they'd escaped from their places when no one was looking and then rushed to resume them.

Eden shivered. She was starting to feel what he was feeling: fine drops of water landing on her head and shoulders. "Rain," she said softly, smiling back. It was the first rainfall of her life.

"Here we are," Sasha announced.

They'd arrived at a massive four-story stucco

building. It was bigger than some of the mansions Eden had granted wishers. Her jaw dropped. "This is your *house*?"

Sasha laughed. "This is an *apartment complex*. We live in *one* of these apartments."

Eden felt her cheeks flush. "Right," she muttered. She followed them through the parking lot. They reached one of the doors, and Tyler pulled a key out from under the welcome mat.

"Home sweet home," Sasha said as the door swung open.

The room they stepped into was dull, dreary, and full of junk. A dust-colored sofa and recliner were home to a collection of unopened mail, surf magazines, catalogs, and clothes. Empty glasses and plastic bottles crowded next to one another on a coffee table. There was no art on the bland white walls, no décor, no other furniture in the room except a large flat-screen TV. Eden thought of the lamp's sitting room, with its polished hardwood floor and plush armchairs. In terms of style and comfort, she had to admit it was a step up from this. Still, the mellow hues of twilight streamed through a glass pane on the front wall. You couldn't beat the view through a bona fide window.

"Sorry it's such a mess," Tyler said. "It's not usually like this."

"Yes it is!" Sasha laughed. She walked through a door into the kitchen. It was a disaster too. The tile floor was dingy, the sink overflowed with dirty dishes, and the trash can was so stuffed with rubbish, its lid was propped open, its contents on display.

At the square kitchen table sat a thin, mournful man with sloppy salt-and-pepper hair. He didn't even look up from the newspaper in his hands.

"What's up, Dad?" Sasha said. The man's eyes, weighed down by enormous bags, flitted up at them momentarily. "This is Eden," she continued. "She's going to spend the night."

The man murmured in acknowledgment but offered nothing more. Sasha motioned with her head for Eden to follow her out.

"Sorry about him," she said as she led Eden down a short hall. "He's—"

"He's fine," said Tyler defensively. "Just tired and overworked."

"Anyway," Sasha said, "our room." She opened a door at the end of the hall to a bedroom bisected by a thick white curtain. Unlike the other rooms in the apartment, this one had personality—rather, *two* personalities.

On the right side, a rumpled blue-and-red plaid cover was splayed across the unmade bed. Above it was a poster of a girl on a surfboard with a perfect wave arching above her. Sneakers and clothes were scattered all over the floor.

On the other wall were framed photos of girls in matching uniforms that Eden supposed were for sports teams. Trophies competed for space on a high wooden dresser, but in front of them all was a framed photo of a pretty woman with high cheekbones holding a baby in one arm, with a toddler-size Tyler on her lap. The photographer had captured her mid-laugh, so lines of happiness creased the corners of her eyes.

On the other side of the curtain, the left half of the room was immaculate. The precisely made bed was covered with a wrinkle-free slate-gray comforter. A black-and-white poster of a rock star hung over it. Eden recognized him; he was a prominent figure in American pop culture who'd found the lamp and summoned Cadence in 1988. Unfortunately, he was the victim of a foolishly worded wish. He'd gotten his place in history, but had died before the age of thirty. His name was Kurt Cobain.

Hanging on the wall across from the bed were four wooden boards, about thirty inches long by eight inches wide, covered in hand-painted designs. Another board, just like them but fitted with four small wheels on the bottom, leaned against the corner.

On the wall alongside the bed hung two framed

photos. One was of Sasha, barefoot and radiant, sitting on a car trunk eating an ice cream cone. The other was of Tyler, Cameron, and Devin, standing on a bench on the boardwalk with their hands on their hips.

Including both sides of the curtain, the room was smaller than Eden's closet. Her wardrobe wouldn't even have fit inside.

Sasha pulled the lamp out of her beach bag and dropped the bag on the floor. She handed Eden a T-shirt and shorts. "Put these on," she instructed. "We'll go make dinner."

In the kitchen, Tyler and Sasha assembled a smorgasbord of junk food extracted from colorful packages. They cleared space to sprawl on the sofa and shoved aside cups on the coffee table to make room for their feast. Sasha set the lamp atop a tall stack of magazines. Their dad had retreated to his room, so they were free to discuss things openly, though Eden wondered if he'd even have noticed if he were still there.

She reached into the red bag and pulled out one of the chips. "Wow," she said as she chewed it. "These are *really* cheesy."

"You don't have Doritos in Sweden?" Tyler asked.

"*Duh.* They eat meatballs," Sasha said. "Right?"

"Among other things." Eden took a sip from the red can they'd handed her. *Coca-Cola*, the side read in cursive. The sweet, fizzy drink burned her throat when she swallowed. She blinked back tears, and her eyes landed on the flat-screen. "Can we turn on the TV?"

Tyler pushed a button on the remote control and the screen lit up. A middle-aged woman with teased hair and shiny skin was ballroom dancing with a man half her age. He leaned her into a low dip.

"Nope," Tyler said, pressing another button.

Sasha reached across Eden to try to take the remote from him. "I *like* that show!"

"No chance," he said. Eden watched, transfixed, as the screen flitted from the dancers to a close-up of a blue macaw to a bride in a wedding gown sprinting across a grass lawn. What *were* all these programs? Xavier had covered television briefly and dismissively, calling it "the ultimate showcase of human depravity." Eden had only snatched glances of it on a couple grantings. She hadn't realized it provided so many *options*.

"What do *you* want to watch, Eden?" Sasha asked. Eden shook her head, dumbfounded by the number of images flickering across the screen. "Do you like dancing?" she went on hopefully.

"What's this?" Tyler had stopped on a shot of a shlubby man in a grease-stained T-shirt. He was gesturing toward a team of men shoveling hot chips down a spiral staircase.

On a blue bar that ran across the bottom of the screen read the words *Australian man cleans up 'hot mess.'*

"What on Earth!" Sasha leaned forward on the couch.

Darryl Dolan looked into the camera. "I'm not surprised this happened," he said. "All my life I've been an unlucky man." He picked up a handful of hot chips and shoved them in his mouth.

Eden giggled. She wished she could tell Sasha and Tyler the whole story.

"And now, a breaking story for those of us right here in San Diego County." The shot changed to a man and a woman sitting behind a large desk in front of a cityscape. "President Porter has announced an unexpected trip to Southern California." A photo of a woman with neat white hair wearing a pressed navy suit appeared on the screen. She couldn't have been any younger than seventy, but there was still a bright spark in her eyes.

"No way!" Sasha said. "She's coming *here*?"

Eden remembered learning about this female president. Her election was a milestone in American history.

"After the final day of the UN Climate Summit tomorrow, the president will fly from New York to San Diego. The reason for her visit has not yet been announced."

"Cool," Tyler said.

"*Cool?*" Sasha repeated. "It's *amazing*." She turned to Eden. "Do you know much about President Porter?"

"A little."

"In less than two years, she's accomplished more than most presidents do in a whole term—or two."

"Chill out," Tyler said, settling back with a chocolate chip cookie. He turned to Eden. "Sasha wants to be the second female president."

"Maybe *that* should be one of our wishes," Sasha said dreamily.

Beep!

The noise was loud and electronic-sounding, and it was followed by a quick rustle.

"Did you hear that?" Tyler said. He muted the TV, but no other sound followed.

"I heard it too," Sasha admitted. On the sofa, she hugged her legs closer.

"It came from outside," Tyler said, getting up and going to the window. "Not far away."

Eden got up too. The two of them peered through the blinds of the window.

In the darkness, all she could make out was the hedge directly below. Besides that, nothing.

Eden pondered that. Tyler had thought he'd heard someone before. But obviously it wasn't Xavier—and who else would follow them?

"Must be nothing," Tyler said—but he didn't sound convinced.

"Oh my gosh." Sasha's eyes had grown big. "*Tyler.* How did we not think of this before?"

"Think of what?" Tyler said without turning around. He was peeking through the blinds again, still preoccupied by whatever was outside the window.

"What we can wish for! Tyler, think about it!"

He turned around and faced her. It was almost as if Eden could see their minds align.

"Mom," he said in a whisper.

Sasha nodded emphatically.

"Oh my God. Okay." He sat on the couch next to her, grabbed the lamp, and closed his eyes.

"Wait," Eden said, still standing in front of them. She was desperate to delay him. Her time on Earth was slipping away as quickly as sand through fingers. "Don't you think—"

"I wish our mom was still alive!" Tyler said breathlessly.

Eden's heart sank like a stone in water. It was not a wish she'd expected.

Tyler opened his eyes, and both of them stared at the lamp in anticipation. Sasha was squeezing Tyler's forearm so tightly her fingertips were white.

Eden swallowed. The second rule had saved her. Tyler had made an ungrantable wish. But of course, they didn't know that. As Eden's heart rate returned to normal, Tyler and Sasha waited in tense silence for about thirty seconds.

Finally, Sasha spoke softly. "Ty, I don't think it worked."

"I should have known!" Tyler punched the sofa cushion beside him. He blinked several times, and his jaw muscle pulsed.

Sasha watched him worriedly. "Ty—" she began, but he jumped up and bolted down the hall. Sasha got up and ran after him.

Eden had denied wishes of resurrecting loved ones before, but she'd never known the wishers well enough to wonder what the people had meant to them. She'd never had a reason to care. As she sat alone on the dust-colored couch, she realized that in the past few hours, that had changed. The emotion that had flashed across Tyler's face was a lot like Sasha's when her ankle was sprained. But this time Eden couldn't fix it.

Eden could hear murmurs of them talking from the bedroom. She'd been hit by a strange affliction of her own: she was jealous. Whatever they were feeling, they were feeling it together. They shared a bond she'd never known—and never could know as long as she was a genie.

Eden looked at the lamp, sitting on a stack of magazines. Xavier and Goldie would have seen the whole exchange through the telescope. They were probably livid. As a genie, it was her duty to tell Tyler his wish hadn't come true because of the second rule's restriction. But she hadn't told them about the rules. They didn't even know she was one with the power to grant their wishes.

She was violating more and more of the lamp's rules. If she ever went back, she was going to get an epic scolding—and Xavier would probably make her write a book about all the things she'd done wrong.

Sasha crept back into the living room.

"Sorry about that," she said, sitting next to Eden. Her eyes were pink and puffy.

"That's okay," Eden said.

They sat in silence for a moment. Then:

"She died eight months ago. Last year on Christmas Eve."

Goose bumps rose on Eden's arms. That wasn't long ago at all.

"She wasn't sick when we were little. They only diagnosed it a year before that." She shook her head. "She used to tell us stories," she said. "Fairy tales. With monsters, mermaids, fairies, wizards. Genies." Eden had to look away.

"I guess she'd make them up as she went. I never heard those stories anywhere else." Sasha frowned. "But all that changed when she got sick. She got...mean. Tired. She didn't want to see us. She *looked* different.

She got treatments, and her hair fell out..." Her voice broke, and she stopped talking.

Eden opened her mouth to say something... but she didn't know what, or even where to begin.

"Sorry. I didn't mean to get into all this," Sasha said, rubbing her eyes. "I never talk about it. *We* never do. Me and Tyler. Dad. I mean, you met my dad. He's so out of it, it's almost like we lost him too."

It was true: Mr. Rockwell seemed... well, sort of half-there. In the kitchen he'd had the energy of a statue. It was almost like he wasn't sure he wanted to be alive. She wondered what *he* would have wished for if they'd met under normal circumstances.

Eden had never been around people who'd dealt with this death stuff before. Before coming to Earth, she'd never expected to. Mortality was a messy mystery she did not care to explore.

But when she thought about it, she supposed a lot of mortals would know other mortals who had stopped living. She thought about her wishers. Had the French-woman on the farm ever known someone who'd died? The Brazilian girl, Jade? The old man in Jamaica? Hot chips–loving Darryl?

No way, she thought. They'd been nothing like Mr. Rockwell.

But then again, how would she know?

"I guess it was pretty dumb to think an old oil lamp you found on the beach could bring her back. A genie lamp." Sasha laughed weakly. "What were we thinking?"

Part of Eden felt terribly guilty. And yet, if Sasha and Tyler thought the lamp was an old, unenchanted piece of junk, they wouldn't try to make any more wishes. Which meant she could stay on Earth indefinitely. Was it wrong to be glad about that?

"It *is* strange that my foot healed today. I guess it must have been a fluke. Who knows." Sasha shrugged sadly. "Anyway. We should probably get to bed. We've got to be up early in the morning." She tried to smile. "Your first day of school in America. Are you excited?"

"*Yes!*" Eden couldn't restrain herself.

Sasha laughed in disbelief. "You're a strange girl, you know that?" She shook her head. "I hope no one gives you trouble."

That night, Eden lay on an inflatable mattress Sasha had extracted from an overstuffed closet. Its shape shifted unreliably and its scratchy sheets were a far cry from the 600 thread count she was used to. But then again, hours earlier she hadn't even known if she'd be sleeping under a roof tonight. It would do.

She shifted from her back to her stomach, then fluffed her flat pillow and laid her head down again.

She sighed and looked at the time on Sasha's digital clock: 1:34 A.M. It was strange to spend a night without Xavier's army of clocks marking the hours as they passed.

What would Xavier and Goldie be doing right now? Were they panicking, thinking of ways to get her back?

It seemed like it was true that only one of them could leave the lamp. That was one thing Xavier hadn't lied about, at least. Not that it mattered. Eden couldn't believe how he'd deceived her. Her whole life he'd been taking trips to Earth while she spent hours dreaming of a way there. And Goldie had been in on it, too!

It was a good thing she'd escaped. She wouldn't have been able to live with them another day. She could never trust them again.

Yes, she concluded, in spite of Earth's challenges, she was much better off here than in that stuffy lamp. On her first day she'd eaten in a restaurant, swum in the ocean, and made mortal friends. It had been the best day of her life.

A wave of exhaustion hit her. Sure, she had a lot to figure out here on Earth. But so far she was doing just fine. And tomorrow, she'd start school—exactly like a mortal twelve-year-old would. Nothing could be better.

Satisfied, she finally made peace with the air mattress and drifted off to sleep.

Twelve

Noel was fifteen minutes from heading into court when she received the message from the lamp.

She set aside the documents she'd been reviewing, closed the door of her penthouse corner office, and instructed her assistant to hold her calls. Noel was one of London's top litigators, but lamp business took precedence over everything. Careers on Earth came and went, but matters of the lamp were eternal.

Most likely, it would be Goldie sharing a new shortbread recipe. And yet, even casual correspondence took priority. She owed everything she was to the lamp and its masters.

She unrolled the parchment. As she watched the message, the blood drained from her face.

As was her nature, she responded immediately by snapping into action. She unlocked a secret drawer in her desk, extracted a cell phone reserved exclusively for lamp affairs, and dialed her best friend.

"*Oh my God!*" Tabitha exploded when she answered. "Can you *believe* this? I'm in shock!"

The message must have gone to all loyal alumni. "Pull yourself together," Noel said tersely. "We have to act quickly and intelligently."

"An escape from the lamp!" Tabitha marveled. "I never thought I'd see the day. That's one gutsy little genie."

Noel had to agree. After granting for mortals like Christopher Columbus and then spending more than five hundred years on Earth, she thought she'd seen it all. But *this*—this was truly inconceivable. "Tab, I think we've got to go to San Diego."

"I think you're right. Gosh, it's sort of exciting, isn't it?"

"You could say that." Noel's phone beeped with an incoming call. "I've got Genevieve coming in on the other line."

"And I've got Ivy," Tabitha said.

"Let's take them. Call you back."

In the sitting room of her home in South Africa, Tabitha switched over to Ivy's call. "Can you believe it?"

"Hardly." Ivy's voice always sounded far away, like she was phoning from another planet.

"What do we do?"

"Bola's got a plan."

"Of course she does."

"But we all need to get there—and fast."

"I'll book a ticket." Tabitha paused. "Do you think *they* know?"

"There's no telling," Ivy said.

"Because if they do..."

"Let's not even think about it."

They hung up, and Ivy sat in silence for a moment. She looked out toward the Gullfoss waterfall, one of Iceland's most well-known natural wonders. She'd been at her favorite café, drinking tea and working on a sonnet, when the message arrived from the lamp. Ivy had been living in Iceland for the past twelve years, enjoying the stunning landscape and dabbling in poetry and painting. The news from Xavier and Goldie had been the first interruption in her peaceful life for quite some time.

Ivy's phone rang. It was Bola. She was taking the lead, as usual.

"Talk to me," Ivy said. She sipped her tea and listened to the plan.

Thirteen

To Eden, Ms. Celeste Mattris did not look qualified to administer either guidance or counseling. She wore a hot-pink blazer and a matching knee-length skirt. Her rubbery lips were unnaturally puffy, and her eyelashes were unthinkably long. She reeked so strongly of perfume, Eden nearly sneezed when she stepped inside her office. But Tyler had said that as Mission Beach Middle School's guidance counselor, Ms. Mattris alone had the power to make her an official student. Eden was determined not to jeopardize that. So the next morning, as Ms. Mattris read the note she'd brought in, Eden folded her hands in her lap, breathed through her mouth, and set her mind to getting through the meeting with no complications.

"Eden Johansson?" Ms. Mattris asked, looking up.

"That's my name." Eden tried to sound natural.

"So you've just moved from Sweden." Ms. Mattris

tapped her fingernails on the surface of her desk. They were extremely long, squared at the ends, and, like her outfit, a plastic-looking pink. Upon closer inspection, Eden saw that three rhinestones adorned the end of each nail.

According to Tyler and Sasha, the school required a number of documents for admission. Without at least a note from her mother, they'd said, she wouldn't be able to enroll. So that morning at the kitchen table, she'd forged a letter while they told her exactly what to write.

Ms. Mattris blinked in her direction. "It says here that all your documents were lost with your luggage?"

"Yeah. But I'm hoping I'll get them back soon."

"They're very important."

"I know," Eden said earnestly. "But I really don't want to miss the first day of school."

Ms. Mattris removed her cat's-eye glasses. "Are you up to speed on math?"

Eden frowned. Xavier was currently covering calculus. She'd learned algebra as a child, before her granting years had started. "I think so," she said.

Ms. Mattris pouted as she typed on the computer in front of her. In the office was a bookshelf, but unlike the fully stocked shelves in the lamp's lesson room, not a single book was on it. Instead, it was filled with things Eden assumed must be special tools for the profession of guidance counseling: a number of stuffed animals, a glass display case exhibiting a sparkly tiara nestled in crushed velvet, and several framed photos of a teacup poodle dressed in various outfits. Each item perplexed her, but the photos were especially puzzling. She hadn't realized dogs ever wore clothes; she'd been under the impression it was normal for them to walk around naked.

"History." Ms. Mattris looked at Eden blankly. "You know much about history?"

"Ancient or modern?" Eden asked. "We've covered both, of course, but I haven't brushed up on the Bronze Age or the Iron Age in a few years. I'm a little rusty on the Sumerian Renaissance, the Shang dynasty, the Trojan War—"

"That's fine." Ms. Mattris reached into a drawer and pulled out something small and round that looked like chocolate. "You want a brownie bite?" Eden politely declined. Ms. Mattris sighed. "I'm gonna get so fat this year," she said mournfully before shoving it between her lips.

"Geography," she said through a chocolaty mouthful. "Well, you lived in Europe, so..." She swallowed and jabbed the keys on her keyboard.

Eden was confused, but said nothing. Sasha and Tyler had coached her to keep as quiet as possible, and she was determined not to mess up. Leaning down, she unzipped the denim backpack Sasha had let her borrow, along with the red pleated skirt, white T-shirt, and brown sandals she was wearing. She slipped her fingers inside the backpack. There, next to a notebook half filled with Tyler's history notes from last year, was the lamp's cool metal. Even though she had no desire to go back inside, knowing it was with her was comforting. Somehow, leaving it at the Rockwells' apartment hadn't felt right.

"English," Ms. Mattris said. She placed her glasses back on her nose and squinted through them. "Have you read many books?"

Eden rezipped the backpack and returned her hands to her lap. "Nearly everything regarded as a classic, I think. All the Pulitzer winners, all the Man Booker winners—"

"Fine," Ms. Mattris said. She'd flipped open a compact and was inspecting herself in its mirror. She patted the pile of bronze-colored curls on top of her head. "Ever written an essay?"

Now Eden was really confused. Was this a trick question? "Yes…"

"Perfect." Ms. Mattris snapped her compact closed with finality, as if that were the question she'd been leading up to all along. "You'll fit right in." She typed a bit more, and the printer behind her spat out a white sheet. Ms. Mattris rolled over to it in her chair and handed it to Eden. "Your schedule."

"Thank you!" Eden stood up.

"Have a great year!" Ms. Mattris called as she left. Then she said, wistfully: "Seventh grade was my favorite."

Sasha and Tyler were waiting by the office's reception desk.

"All good?" Tyler asked.

"Mission Beach Middle has a brand-new student," Eden answered proudly.

Sasha snatched the schedule from her. "Homeroom, Spanish, World History, Science, Lunch, Math, P.E., English . . . We're in all the same classes!"

Eden couldn't stop smiling. She was officially a student in a school full of mortals!

"Hello, Tyler. Girls," boomed a voice from above. She tilted her head to see a giant man with a gray-blond crew cut and an unusually wide jaw. "Why are *we* in the office this morning?"

"How could we know why *you*—" Eden started, but Tyler cut her off.

"Good morning, Principal Willis. This is Eden," he said. "She just moved here from Sweden. Ms. Mattris helped us enroll her in classes."

"Welcome back, Sasha," the man said. "You." He faced Eden. *"Du har precis flyttat hit från Sverige?"*

So this man, whoever he was, would be Eden's first challenge. *You've just moved here from Sweden?* he'd asked.

Naturally, Xavier had taught the recent unit on her alleged homeland in the native language. Eden's Swedish was fluid and sure. *"Jag kom precis hit,"* she answered. For the first time, she was truly grateful for Xavier's demanding curriculum.

"Jag är född i Stockholm." The man smiled icily. *I was born in Stockholm,* he'd said. "I'm Principal Willis. Welcome to my school." He clasped hands the size of dinner plates in front of him. "Now, off to class. Don't be late on your first day."

Sasha and Tyler led the way down a hallway packed with throngs of students sporting new clothes and summer tans. Suddenly, a piercing ring sent students skittering in every direction. Eden jumped at the noise, then searched frantically for its source. She knew alarms were used to alert mortals to emergencies. But after a moment she realized the other students had barely reacted. Tyler shook his head, laughing.

"Better get used to that," he said. "Starting today, it runs your life."

"Don't you have that in Sweden?" Sasha asked. "The bell rings to start and end classes. That was the warning bell. Meaning we have one minute to get to homeroom."

Tyler grinned. "Don't look so scared. It'll only encourage them."

"Tyler!" Sasha scolded.

He laughed and clapped a hand on her shoulder.

"Good luck. You're gonna need it." A guy walked up and grabbed him round the neck, and he disappeared into the crowd.

"Let's run!" Sasha said. There was no time to be nervous. Eden raced after her to homeroom.

Fourteen

Even though she'd traveled to places on Earth that many mortals would never see, Mission Beach Middle School held countless wonders for Eden. Each time the bell rang, you got to get out of your seat, walk *down the hall* while speaking freely to other students, and proceed into a brand-new classroom to be instructed by a different teacher. This happened *six times* in a school day. Compared to solitary lessons in the lamp, the setup was glorious.

Surprises awaited her in every class. In homeroom, she was shocked when the teacher turned on the TV. She couldn't imagine what Xavier would say about *that*.

On the screen, a teenage boy and girl sat at a desk like the anchors on the news the night before.

"Good morning, and welcome back!" said the boy with a big, cheesy smile. "This is *Mission Beach High*

Morning News, bringing you the local, national, and global news you want to know!"

"If you're new," the girl chimed in, "we broadcast to Mission Beach High, Middle, and Elementary schools every morning from Monday to Friday.

"The season opener for our Mission Beach High Tigers is Friday night, at home," she said. "Tickets are going fast, so make sure you get one!"

"And this afternoon, our middle school football team will be playing a preseason scrimmage against Mount Carmel," the boy added. "Come on out and support your baby Tigers!"

Eden watched in awe as they moved on to local news: a convenience store robbery, the birth of a panda in the San Diego Zoo, the upcoming visit from the president. They even did a spot on the Darryl Dolan story, which seemed to be a media favorite.

After homeroom, Eden and Sasha moved to their first period, Spanish. The teacher was an exhausted-looking woman named Mrs. Cantrell. Her weakly delivered lesson didn't even compare to the dynamic teaching of Xavier. Eden had always known he was brilliant, but in a vague, general way, like the way she knew he had dark hair and loved show tunes. Now she could see how extraordinary he was. Mortals had nothing on him.

As the hour went on, Eden couldn't help but wonder what these mortals had *done* in their previous years of schooling. After going over a few basic conversational phrases, they moved on to conjugating simple verbs. To Eden, the lesson was child's play.

But while she was miles ahead academically, there were also parts of school on Earth she didn't understand. Throughout first period, the whole room turned to stare every time she answered a question. A few of the looks she got were downright hostile, but Eden couldn't work out why.

Eventually, Mrs. Cantrell told her to raise her hand.

"Raise my *hand*? Why?"

"Sorry," Sasha spoke up. "She's from Sweden. Things are different there." With her eyes wide, she shook her head emphatically at Eden. So Eden kept her mouth shut through the rest of the class and observed. It seemed students lifted one arm if they wanted to answer a question, and then the teacher chose one of them to speak. It was a peculiar system.

During the class change, Sasha administered a rapid-fire tutorial on classroom etiquette.

"And even if you know the answer—well, you don't always have to say it," she explained, snapping open the lock on her locker. Eden stood next to her in front of the locker she'd been assigned. She had no idea what to do with it.

"Why not?" Eden inspected the mysterious lock; she'd never seen one before. Sasha reached over and spun the dial on the front one way and then the other.

"Well," she said. The lock popped open and Eden hopped back, startled. "Nobody likes a show-off. You do want to make friends, right?"

Eden's skin went cold. "They don't like me?" She hated the way her voice quivered, but she felt like she'd been punched in the stomach. Mortals were simple, with simple thoughts and desires. Before, when she came to Earth for grantings, she'd never cared what they thought of her. She knew she was above them, and she was never going to be there long anyway. But for the first time in her life, she was planning to stay for a while. For the first time, she cared what they thought.

Sasha seemed to think hard about how to answer. "Right now I don't think anyone knows *what* to think of you."

Eden felt as vulnerable as a toddler. She tucked a wisp of pale hair behind her ear. Suddenly she wasn't sure of anything—not even the clothes she was wearing. She'd assumed posing as a mortal would be easy. After all, she was better than them, right?

"Nerd alert!" someone called. Eden looked up to see a petite, well-groomed girl strutting by. Her thick, curly brown hair was pulled half up, and she wore a long-sleeved baby pink dress. Skye and Claire flanked her like sidekicks. At the insult, each of them was overcome by giggles.

The girl smirked at Eden, showing dimples in her cheeks. She'd been behind one of the hostile looks in Spanish class.

"Grow up!" Sasha shot back. Then, "Skye? Claire? Hel-*lo*?"

The girls walked on without acknowledging her.

Sasha looked disconcerted. To Eden, she said, "I don't even know who that girl is. I think she's new too."

"Seems like she's doing better than I am," Eden said despondently. "Why are your friends with her?"

"I don't know." Sasha shook her head, as if trying to forget it. "We've got to get going. Are you gonna carry that backpack around all day?" Eden realized Sasha had stored her own backpack inside her locker, taking only a notebook and pencil. Even though the bracelet would ensure no one could take the lamp from her, the thought of being apart from it made her anxious. But after all, there was a lock. And she *did* need to blend in better.

With new determination, she shoved her backpack inside and slammed her locker closed. "I'll show those mortals I'm just like them," she declared.

Sasha blinked. "Those what?"

Eden flushed. "Sorry. People."

Sasha seemed to consider saying something, but

changed her mind. She glanced at the clock on the wall. "Come on," she said. "We've got two minutes to get to the other side of the building."

As they rushed down the hall, Eden scolded herself. *Mortals*. A small but revealing slip.

She had to start being more careful.

When Eden and Sasha walked into second period, there was no teacher in sight. Back-to-school chatter filled the air as students milled around.

But when the bell rang, the party ended abruptly. A woman with skin so black it almost gleamed blue came striding in. She had high, regal cheekbones, blinding white teeth, and tight red dreadlocks wound in a bun on top of her head. Her limbs were long and powerful, like they belonged to an Olympic hurdler. She pivoted at the front of the room and faced them, shoulders back and chin tilted high.

Her gaze was cold enough to freeze water.

"Sit," the woman hissed. A reverent hush filled the room. Anyone who was still standing sat quickly. The woman lifted her chin even higher and eyed them imperiously. "I am Ms. Bola." Her voice was low, with a sharp British accent. She enunciated each word, leaving pockets of space between them to build suspense. "Today we begin our study of world history."

How many times had Eden studied that face, drawn

by Goldie's pen with incredible accuracy? She could rattle off the genie's career highlights on cue. There was no doubt in her mind: this was the very same Bola from the Lamp History course guide.

What was she doing at the front of this classroom? Bola was one of the most esteemed genies of all time. Xavier and Goldie exchanged messages with her often, many of which Eden had seen. She seemed to remember that after several centuries in Eastern Europe, Bola had recently moved to San Francisco. That would only be a short plane ride away.

But what could possibly make her want to teach seventh graders at Mission Beach Middle?

Ms. Bola read through the names for roll call impatiently, barely pausing long enough for each student to respond. When she reached Eden's, she raised her head like a serpent seeking her prey.

Eden swallowed. "Here," she said.

Ms. Bola smiled. *"Eden,"* she said with unnatural warmth. "Like the garden. The original paradise."

An uneasy feeling came over Eden.

"Ms. Mattris told me you just moved here from Sweden. Is that right?"

Eden gulped. "Yes."

"Wonderful." Ms. Bola gave her a chilling smile. "I'm sure there are *many* things you can teach us."

Over the following thirty minutes of her sweeping

introduction to world history, Ms. Bola called on Eden no fewer than seventeen times—not one of which Eden raised her hand for—to share facts about Sweden and its history. She practically ignored the other students, which seemed to suit them just fine. They sat shell-shocked at their desks, terrified the teacher's attention would turn. Fortunately, Xavier's unit on Sweden was fresh in Eden's mind, so she kept up and answered every question correctly.

Between questions, Eden tried to figure out what was going on. Naturally, Ms. Bola knew who she was. Eden was sure she'd made an appearance in at least one of the messages Xavier and Goldie had sent to her.

Could she have come purposely to find her?

Finally Ms. Bola announced that she was going to play something on the TV. She instructed them to pay close attention. When she turned off the lights, Eden sighed and sank down in her seat, grateful to be off the hook.

On the screen, President Porter was speaking at a podium. Behind her was a white wall printed with the words *Climate Summit*. It was, Eden realized, where Xavier had been when she'd looked through the telescope in the study.

"We live in a beautiful world," the woman said. Her clear, keen eyes peered out from soft, lined skin. "But in order to keep it that way, we've got to learn to treat it well. It's only when you brighten the world that you can truly see its beauty."

Eden smiled. She was glad to see the president wasn't dense and self-serving like most mortals. She had to admit, some mortals did manage to surprise her. In her dreams of Earth, it was one thing she'd never seen coming.

Ms. Bola turned on the classroom lights.

"Eden. Has a female prime minister ever been elected in Sweden?"

Eden blinked. "No, although Sweden is known as one of the world's most progressive nations in gender equality. A lot of people expected Anna Lindh, who served as minister for foreign affairs, to become the first female prime minister, but she was assassinated in September 2003."

Ms. Bola clapped slowly. "Impressive. Xavier would be proud."

"What did you say?" Eden gasped.

A sly smile flashed across Ms. Bola's face. "I said your teachers would be proud."

But Eden knew what she'd heard.

"Spend the rest of the period writing a paper on your reaction to the speech we just heard. Due at the beginning of class tomorrow." Ms. Bola fixed that withering stare directly on her. "Except for Eden. I need to speak to you in the hall." She nodded. "Come with me." Reluctantly, Eden followed her out of the classroom.

Up close, Bola was at once terrifying to behold, and so beautiful it was hard to look away. Though she appeared to be no older than thirty, Eden knew she'd been on Earth for more than two thousand years.

Bola placed long-fingered hands on her hips. Her nails shone like polished walnut shells. "Tell me, Eden. How's Earth treating you?"

Eden swallowed. "What do you mean?"

"Don't play dumb," Bola snapped. "I know how things work in the lamp. You know exactly who I am." She pushed up one cuff of her silk button-down. On her wrist was a gold cuff bracelet, identical to Eden's but deactivated.

"Okay," Eden said carefully. "You're a genie alum."

Bola's eyes rolled slowly in their sockets. "Obviously." She shook her head. "What were you thinking? How *dare* you run away from your duties?"

"Hey!" Eden put her own hands on her hips. "I'm the one who should be asking questions. What are you doing here?"

Bola rolled her eyes again. "For a genie, you're a little slow, you know that?"

"Tell me!"

"I came for you." Bola let that sink in for a moment.

"To make sure you get back in the lamp before you do serious damage."

"How did you know I left?"

Bola seemed impatient. "Xavier and Goldie sent me a message asking for help. Since they can't come get you themselves."

For a split second, Eden was touched. They must really miss her if they'd enlisted alumni for help.

"They messaged all the loyal alumni."

"The *loyal* alumni? What does that mean?"

Bola's eyes widened. Eden had a feeling she hadn't meant to say that word.

"What happened with the alumni who aren't loyal?" she demanded. "The ones they don't communicate with?"

"Forget about that. The important thing is—"

But Eden was tired of having her questions brushed away. All at once, she remembered that sense of betrayal when she'd caught Xavier in the spout. She remembered, once again, how he'd lied to her all those years. How he'd kept her confined, like a pet in a cage, when he knew all she wanted was freedom.

"I've got bad news—for them, and for you." She stared Bola straight in the eyes. "Because I'm never, ever, ever going back."

Bola's dark eyes narrowed to slits. It was not what she'd expected to hear. "How dare you," she breathed. "It is an *honor* to be a genie. It is *sacred*."

"Not for me!" Eden shot back. "I didn't choose it, and I won't do it anymore. Just like I told Xavier." Her heart was pounding, but she wouldn't be scared into surrender.

Just then, a figure rounded the corner. Over Bola's shoulder, Eden recognized its hulking shape: Principal Willis.

Unaware that he was coming, Bola stalked toward Eden, more venomous than before. "Do you realize you're jeopardizing the whole granting system? In thousands of years, a genie has *never* done something like this."

"What's going on here?" Mr. Willis thundered as he approached.

Bola gave Eden one more death glare, then turned to face him.

"Who are you?" he barked.

"We haven't officially met. I am Ms. Bola." She extended a hand. He took it hesitantly. In spite of his tank-like stature, Bola seemed to strike as much awe in him as she did in the seventh graders.

"Are you teaching a class at my school?"

"Yes. The superintendent hired me this morning."

The corners of Mr. Willis's mouth turned down. "Mrs. Melvin is gone? But she's been with us for fourteen years."

"Very unfortunate," Ms. Bola said stiffly. "I don't know the details."

Suddenly, Mr. Willis noticed Eden. His pale eyes locked on her. "Well, well! Our Swedish import!" He tilted his head. "Why were you two out here in the hall? Was there a behavioral problem?"

"Not at all," Ms. Bola said. "We were just having a chat." She shot Eden a saccharine smile.

"Sweden, what do you think of our American school?"

Eden squirmed. "It's good."

"Är det svårt att hänga med på lektionerna på engelska?" Is it difficult to keep up with lessons in English?

"Jag kan hantera det," she said. *I'm managing.*

With that, the sound of the bell cut through the air. Students burst through the door like jack-in-the-boxes—but slowed their pace as they passed Mr. Willis.

"Time to move." Willis turned to Bola. "You were done with Sweden here, right?"

Bola gritted her teeth. "I guess we'll finish our conversation later." Her lips stretched to show a sinister semblance of a smile. "I'm not going anywhere."

Fifteen

Third period was science. Like in Spanish, the material was incredibly basic; the teacher, a nervous, fortyish man named Mr. Watson, was only beginning to introduce the structure of cells. Again, Eden wondered what these mortals had been doing in school for the past six years. But after what had happened with Bola, it was sort of a relief to be bored. She kept her mouth shut and raised her hand only occasionally.

However, as Mr. Watson began to explain animal cells, Eden felt a sharp poke in her back. *"Ow!"* she cried.

Mr. Watson turned from his drawing of a mitochondrion on the dry-erase board. "Is there a problem?"

Eden glanced over her shoulder. There, at the desk behind her, was the girl from the hallway who'd called her a nerd. The girl smirked, and her dimples appeared.

Eden turned back around. "No problem," she said.

Mr. Watson returned to his drawing. From the desk to her left, Sasha gave her a sympathetic look.

"Loser," the girl whispered, softly, so Mr. Watson couldn't hear. The sharp thing jabbed Eden between the shoulder blades again. This time when she turned around, she saw it was the tip of a paper folded into a small triangle. Grinning, the girl offered it to her. Eden took it and unfolded it discreetly on her desk.

Drawn in pencil on the lined notebook paper was a caricature of Mr. Watson. Big buckteeth protruded over his bottom lip; sweat stains reached from under his arms to his waist; and his pants stopped halfway between his knees and his ankles. In a speech bubble were the words *Science is my life!*

The girl kicked Eden hard in the heel. *"Ow,"* Eden said again—louder this time. Mr. Watson whipped back around.

"What's the problem now?" he said, coming toward her. She was in the second row, so there was no time to hide the paper. He swiped it off the desk.

When he saw it, sadness washed over his face.

"That isn't mine!" Eden protested. She pointed behind her. "She gave it to me!"

"Ex-*cuse* me?" The girl sounded appalled. "I did *not!*"

"Yes, she did!" Sasha cut in. "I saw it."

Mr. Watson looked from Eden to the drawing.

"I swear!" Eden cried.

"She's lying!" the girl insisted.

Mr. Watson shook his head. "Ladies, this is not the way we're going to start the year." He pointed at Eden, then at the other girl. "Eden, Gigi. Both of you in the hall. You can get your story straight out there."

"*Me?*" the girl exclaimed. "But I didn't do anything!"

"Now!" Mr. Watson's face was turning red.

Eden's chair scraped on the floor when she stood up. Seething, she stalked out of the classroom.

Gigi kept up the guise of being wrongly accused until they were through the door. Once they hit the hall, she doubled over laughing.

"What's funny?" Eden demanded.

"Seeing you get in trouble," the girl said. "You're such a suck-up."

"I am not!"

"Yeah, right. I watched you call out every single answer in Spanish. '*Yo soy* too foreign to raise my hand!'" she mimicked.

"I didn't know, okay?"

Gigi leaned against the wall. "Why don't you go back where you came from? Nobody here likes you."

Once again, insecurity pierced Eden like an arrow. "Yeah, right," she muttered, trying her best to hide it.

"You wanna bet?"

"Aren't you new too?" Eden said. "Why don't you worry about yourself?"

"I'm doing fine. I'm making *friends*. You notice how nobody's talking to you? Because it's obvious you don't belong here."

Eden tried to pretend the words didn't affect her—but she couldn't help wondering if they were true.

Just then the classroom door opened, and Mr. Watson came out.

"Girls," he said, "what happened today was unacceptable." He fiddled with the pencil in his hand. "I should give you both detention. But since you're both new to Mission Beach Middle and I want us to start off on the right foot, I'm only going to give you a warning."

Eden relaxed a little. She didn't know what detention was, but she didn't like the sound of it.

"Next time, this conversation will be with Mr. Willis. And I guarantee he won't be as nice as I am." He looked pointedly at Eden, then Gigi. "Understood?"

"Fine," said Gigi flippantly.

"Eden?"

Eden nodded, silently fuming.

"Now, come rejoin the class."

On the way back in, Gigi stuck her tongue out at Eden.

It was a relief to discover that the next period was lunch. Eden went through the cafeteria line with Tyler and

Sasha. Each of them got a tray of chicken fingers and French fries, and Tyler grabbed a bag of M&M's to split for dessert. Eden still had no money, of course, so he paid for hers again. How would she ever pay them back?

Although Eden and Sasha had been together all morning, it was the first time they'd reconvened with Tyler.

"You surviving so far?" he asked playfully.

"Barely." It wasn't much of an exaggeration. Between her encounter with Bola and the incident in Science, school was becoming much more complicated than she'd expected.

"What happened with you and the world history teacher in the hall?" Sasha asked. "She was so intense."

"Uh-oh. You already got pulled into the hall by a teacher?" Tyler teased.

"Twice," Sasha clarified.

"She was asking about my school back in Sweden," Eden lied.

"She was so fixated on you. It was weird," Sasha said. "You'd think she'd be happy you're so smart."

"Hey, have you heard anything from your mom?" Tyler asked.

"Not yet," Eden said. "She can be sort of hard to pin down."

"Sweden! How goes it in the U.S. of A.?" Cameron and Devin slid into the seats next to Eden and Tyler. Their trays were loaded with chicken fingers.

Eden shrugged. She didn't want to admit how badly things were going.

Even lunch was confusing. In the cafeteria, it was clear to see how students divided into cliques. At least one common trait united each table. One pack of girls wore high heels and lots of makeup. A group of guys had 'hawk hairstyles like the man at the beach. At another table, a black instrument case was stowed by each seat.

Their own group was small—just Eden, the Rockwells, and the two other boys.

"Don't we have more friends?" Devin asked. "Sash, where are your girls?"

"I guess they've made new friends." Sasha nodded toward a table across the cafeteria. Skye and Claire were sitting with a group of boys dressed in matching orange jerseys. One of them had an arm draped around Skye; Claire was laughing at something another had said.

"Hm. I see," said Devin. "The football team."

"Isn't that the other new girl?" Cameron asked.

Sure enough, Gigi was sitting with them too.

"Maybe I should start playing football," Devin joked.

"How do you know who she is? She's a seventh grader," Sasha said.

Cameron shrugged. "Word gets around. I heard she moved here from Arizona."

"Well, she's terrible," Sasha said fiercely. "She's been bullying Eden all day." The conviction in her voice took Eden aback. She hadn't realized Sasha cared so much.

"What did she do?" Tyler asked sharply.

Sasha explained what had happened in Science.

"What are Skye and Claire doing with her?" Cameron asked.

"Showing their true colors, I guess." Sasha dragged a French fry through a mound of ketchup.

As they launched into a conversation about the loyalty of guys versus girls in friendships, it struck Eden that *she* was the reason Skye and Claire weren't sitting with Sasha. They'd disliked Eden from the start, but Sasha had stood up for her. And she didn't even know the truth about who Eden was.

When the bell rang to dismiss lunch, Sasha walked ahead with Cameron and Devin, but Tyler hung back.

"Eden," he said low as he walked beside her, "I hope you're not letting that girl get to you."

She looked at him in surprise. Tyler was far more perceptive than most mortals. And even stranger, he really seemed to care.

"People only treat each other like that if they don't know who they are," he said.

Eden had to look away.

"You know that, right?"

"I guess so." If she was honest with herself, she wasn't sure she knew who *she* was. She'd thought life as a mortal would fit her like a glove; she hadn't expected so many new challenges on Earth.

Her eye caught on her bracelet, and Goldie's words came rushing back. *If you're ever unsure of who you are,* she'd said, *look at your bracelet and remember.*

"Anyway," Tyler said as they reached her locker, "I hope the rest of your day is smooth sailing."

"Trust me, I do too."

But not ten minutes later, the day took another unexpected turn. The teacher in Eden's math class hadn't even made it through roll call when a student came in and handed her a note.

"Eden Johansson?" she said, looking up from it.

"Here!" Roll call was one thing she'd learned to do right.

"No, this note is for you. Your mother is in the office."

The room filled with snickers.

"Mommy misses you!" a boy called in a high voice.

"My mother?" Eden stayed seated, perplexed.

Next to her, Sasha gave her a strange look.

"That's what the note says," the teacher said, glancing down at it again.

Slowly, Eden rose from her desk. Every mortal in the class was staring.

One of them was Gigi. But for once, she wasn't wearing a smug expression. For some reason, she looked just as confused as Eden felt.

Roll call resumed as she squeezed down the aisle of desks.

Though she didn't know what or who to expect in the office, Eden had a feeling it would involve Bola. But when she got there, her world history teacher was nowhere in sight. Instead, in a chair between two angry-looking kids, was a different woman.

She was about thirty years old, slim, and stunning in a tailored mint-green dress. Shiny, honey-colored hair tumbled down her chest, and her catlike eyes were unbearably turquoise.

She looked nothing at all like Bola, yet the sight of her affected Eden the same way. Awe, wonder, and disbelief filled her. She was looking at someone she'd been dreaming about since childhood.

Sylvana rose from her chair as she entered.

"Darling!" she breathed. "How I've missed you!"

The next thing she knew, Sylvana's arms were wrapped around her, pressing Eden's face against her rose-scented neck. Sylvana is hugging me right now, Eden thought dizzily. It was so absurd, she could barely comprehend it.

"Missed me?" was all she could think to say.

"You didn't tell me your mother was coming," boomed Mr. Willis. For such a large man, he really had a knack for appearing out of nowhere.

Eden felt five steps behind.

"*Jag skulle kommit fram igår*," the woman said. *I was supposed to arrive yesterday*—in Swedish.

"What happened?" Mr. Willis asked. "Are you okay?"

"*Du är så snäll. Ingen fara, bara en inställd flygning.*" *You're so kind. Everything's fine, just a canceled flight.* Then she batted her eyelashes at him.

"Thank goodness!" Mr. Willis's voice echoed through the office. "Eden, you must be so relieved to see her!"

Slowly the pieces were coming together. Another alum had arrived—probably to try convincing her to return to the lamp, like Bola had.

But Xavier and Goldie didn't talk to Sylvana. They barely allowed her name to be spoken in the lamp. Why would they send a message to *her*?

Sylvana placed a hand on Mr. Willis's shoulder. "With your permission," she said, "I'd like to check my daughter out of school for the rest of the day."

Mr. Willis's face creased with thought. "Well, technically we need a doctor's note..."

Sylvana's face fell—almost as if she were about to cry. Mr. Willis didn't stand a chance.

"But who am I kidding? You've just come all the way from Sweden!"

"Oh, *thank* you." Sylvana winked. "I promise we'll behave."

Sixteen

When they stepped through the front doors, Eden braced herself for an attack. With no mortals in earshot, Sylvana was sure to snap like Bola had.

But she was wrong. Sylvana stopped and turned Eden to face her. "Let me have a look at you." She looked Eden up and down, taking in her skinny legs and long blond braid. She gasped. "Aren't you beautiful!"

Eden's face grew warm.

"Come on, you must know that. Or do those idiots in the lamp not tell you?" She grinned a million-dollar smile. "Tell me, do you know who I am?"

"You're Sylvana." In the flesh. Eden couldn't believe it.

Sylvana nodded, looking pleased. "That's right."

"But how did you know where to find me?"

Sylvana waved a hand in the air as if that were a minor detail, as pesky as a fly. "I'll explain everything.

Now come on, let's get out of here." She took Eden's hand and led her toward a cherry-red convertible.

By now, Eden had gotten around to doing almost everything Xavier had warned her against. She'd swum in the ocean, made friends with mortals, and nearly lost the lamp. But since her arrival on Earth, she and the Rockwells had walked wherever they went. She still had yet to ride in a car.

She'd seen plenty of them, of course. In the first two years of her career she'd granted a number of wishes for flashy cars with flashy names: Ferrari, Bugatti, Lamborghini. When the vehicles appeared she was always mystified. Sure, they were shiny and sleek. Each one had four wheels and an engine, so it could take you from place to place. But she couldn't understand why mortals fixated on them. When presented with unlimited options, why would you wish for one of these machines?

As if reading her mind, Sylvana said, "You been in one of these things yet?" Eden shook her head. Sylvana's eyes flashed. "You're gonna love it." She held the door open while Eden climbed inside, then sat behind the steering wheel and slid a pair of aviator-style sunglasses onto her nose.

"Ready?"

When Sylvana turned the key in the ignition, the car came to life, purring like a metal beast. Excitedly, Eden gripped the seat. Her heart pounded as they pulled out of the parking lot.

Since she'd never been in a moving car before, she didn't have anything to compare it to. Still, she was pretty sure the way Sylvana drove wasn't legal. She ripped down the road, racing past other cars and sailing through red lights.

Eden closed her eyes. For her, *this* was paradise. She'd never known anything so exhilarating. Finally she understood why mortals wished for these things.

"What do you think?" Sylvana's hair was whipping wildly in the wind.

"Incredible!" Eden yelled. "But where are we going?"

"You'll see." Sylvana jerked the steering wheel for a sharp turn, and Eden noticed her manicured hands. On one wrist was a white-gold watch. Nothing on the other. She wasn't wearing her genie bracelet.

As they cruised down the coast, Eden folded her arms on top of the passenger door and watched the ocean roll by. There was sunshine on her skin, wind in her hair, and no mortals picking on her or alumni nagging her to go back in the lamp. What was so great about school anyway?

Eventually Sylvana turned off the coastal road and drove inland. She pulled the car into a space in a small parking lot.

"This way!" she said, getting out of the car.

This part of San Diego was notably different from the beachy terrain Eden had seen so far. Grass and trees surrounded them, and in the near distance were hills covered in shades of green and brown. Out here, it was much quieter than in Mission Beach.

Sylvana led Eden to a field where a huge nylon parachute, striped with red, yellow, blue, and green, lay spread out and partially inflated on the grass. A stout man with a beard was blasting orange flames from a metal burner into the balloon's mouth. A big woven basket, large enough for several people to stand in, lay sideways next to it, attached by a number of cords.

"Is that a hot air balloon??" Eden squealed.

"Looks like it, doesn't it?" Sylvana crossed her arms and smiled.

"Are we going up in it?"

"Would you like to?" She removed her sunglasses, revealing those blistering blue-green eyes.

"Are you kidding? *Yes!*" Eden rushed up to investigate it more closely.

"Hello, Jerry!" Sylvana said, waving to the bearded man.

He beamed and saluted her. "Hey there! She's nearly ready to go!"

"How did you arrange this?" Eden asked Sylvana in wonder. "Do you live here?"

"*Here?* No!" Sylvana ushered her away so Jerry

couldn't hear. "I've been on Earth for more than six hundred and fifty years," she said. "Long enough to know what to do—and how to do it—in every city."

Eden's mind was spinning. She was desperate to learn all about Sylvana.

"Do you travel much?" she asked.

"All the time! How could you not? There are so many beautiful things to see, so much delicious food to eat, so many gorgeous things to wear..." Sylvana winked. "Life on Earth is *good*."

Eden was bursting with excitement. Finally, someone was validating all the wonderful things she'd suspected about the world—and even better, it was the alum she'd always looked up to!

"All aboard!" Jerry called. The balloon had become so full of air that the basket was sitting upright on the grass. He helped Eden and Sylvana climb over the side, and then he joined them.

"Here we go!" he announced as they lifted off the ground.

Eden leaned over the edge and watched San Diego spread beneath her like a picnic blanket. Houses, roads, cars, and trees all shrank to miniature proportions. From up here she could see how homes were intricately arranged in subdivisions, and how the ground rose and fell to form graceful rolling hills.

She closed her eyes and focused on the feeling of flying. She wanted to remember every second.

When she opened her eyes, Sylvana had produced two ice-cold glass bottles of Coca-Cola. She handed one to Eden, then held out her own to clink against it. She leaned next to her on the basket's woven side, and together they took in the landscape below.

Eden glanced at Jerry, who was on the opposite side of the basket. Piloting the balloon seemed to occupy his attention.

"So where *do* you live?" Eden asked.

"Paris, mostly."

Paris. It was meant to be one of Earth's most wonderful cities.

"Hey, look over there!" Sylvana pointed to the west, where the ocean shimmered magnificently in the distance.

Eden sipped her Coke and marveled at her good fortune. Sylvana was even more fun and carefree than Eden had imagined. Being with her was like being swept up in a wonderful tidal wave. And now that she'd seen how mean and uptight Bola was, her take on immortal life was even more appealing.

"I *knew* you'd be cool," Eden said with satisfaction.

"And I knew *you'd* be cool," Sylvana said. "I mean, look. You're a very special genie. At—what are you, twelve years old?—you've done something no genie has ever done before. You found a way to escape the lamp. You're my *hero*." When Sylvana smiled, her teeth actually seemed to sparkle in the sunlight.

Eden squinted. This had to be a joke. The woman she'd admired her whole life was telling her *she* was *her* hero?

"You're not mad that I escaped?"

"*Mad?* I think you're *brilliant*! If I'd figured out it was possible to leave through the spout, I would have done the same thing in a heartbeat! I was trapped in there for almost sixty years, and spent every day of it dreaming of freedom."

"That's what *I* do," Eden said. Her hunch was right! Sylvana *was* different too.

"I hated it," Sylvana said. "To punish them, I screwed up every wish I ever granted. So much for their little paradise!"

That explained why no wishes were listed in her section of the course guide. Sylvana had probably heard hundreds of lectures like the one after the Darryl Dolan granting.

Sylvana clicked her tongue. "They didn't tell you, did they?"

"They never wanted to talk about you at all."

She rolled her eyes. "Of course they didn't. I'm not surprised. I'm their big, bad secret."

"They said no other genie has been as ungrateful as me. That all the rest of you understood the honor of the position."

"Yeah, all the rest of them did. Except for me. And you." She smirked. "We're two of a kind."

Eden grinned. For the first time, here was someone who understood her.

"Is that why you don't talk to them now?"

"Are you kidding me? When I got out of there, I never wanted to *think* about those two again."

"What about the other alumni they don't talk to? Like Kingsley and Violet. Were they like us too?"

"No, they were good little genies." Sylvana sniffed dismissively. "Doing everything their masters asked. But after they retired and came to Earth, they met me. And I helped them see the light."

"The light?"

"Yeah. You know. The injustice of the whole system." She flipped her honey-colored hair so that it bounced and shone. "See, they say that we're part of a legacy like no other. That part is true. But it's a legacy of oppression. Think about it. Each of us genies is born into captivity and forced to grant idiotic mortals whatever they might desire. We don't get to make decisions about our lives. We're born into slavery. On Earth, that's *illegal*."

Eden had never thought of it quite that way, but she supposed it was true. Much of what Sylvana was saying had run through her mind during lonely hours in the lamp. She'd just never called it what it was.

"Xavier and Goldie are *tyrants*," Sylvana went on. "Not to mention, world-class liars. After I retired, I finally learned about Xavier's little jaunts to Earth. For me, that was the worst lie of all—because he knew how badly I wanted freedom."

That bubbling, burning anger rose up in Eden again. It had been the same for her! She'd never dreamed she'd meet someone who felt the same way.

"Everything you're saying," she said, "is exactly why I left the lamp."

They were flying high now, suspended among the clouds in a dreamy upper layer above the world. In more than one way, Sylvana had given her a whole new perspective.

Sylvana took Eden's empty Coke bottle and set it on the floor. "I just got a great idea." She placed her hands lightly on Eden's shoulders. "Why don't you come with me?"

"With you? Where?"

"Back to Paris! I can show you my life. You'll have a suite in the grandest hotel. I'll show you paintings and sculptures by history's finest artists, and we'll eat the most divine food you've ever tasted."

It was quite an offer: the chance to explore one of

Earth's greatest cities with the woman she'd always longed to meet.

"We'll have so much fun together! It will be like you're really my daughter."

Eden couldn't stop smiling. A few hours ago, her problems had seemed insurmountable. But now that she'd met Sylvana, they were no bigger than the tiny trees and buildings far below.

"Okay," she said. "I'll come."

"You *will?*" Sylvana clasped her hands in delight. She hugged Eden close, so Eden could smell the rose scent on her neck once again. "You're going to love it, I promise."

When the balloon landed, they thanked Jerry and climbed from the basket.

"My private jet is waiting for us at the airport," Sylvana said as she led the way to the parking lot. She pointed a small black device on the key chain at the red convertible, and unlocked the doors with a beep.

"Oh," said Eden, feeling disoriented. "You mean we're going *now?*"

"Why not? We'll stop and get the lamp, and then we'll zip straight over."

Eden frowned. "Did you say the lamp?"

They'd reached the car. Sylvana blinked innocently.

"Well, you don't want to leave it here, do you?"

"I guess not," Eden said hesitantly, climbing in. Why did it matter?

"By the way, where is the lamp?" Sylvana slipped her sunglasses back onto her flawless face.

"In my locker, back at school."

Sylvana winced. "Okay. I guess you'll have to go in and get it. Just make sure to avoid those two kids." With a jerk, she backed the car out of the parking space.

Eden felt uneasy. Taking off for another country without talking to Sasha or Tyler didn't seem right. "Avoid them? Why?"

Sylvana didn't seem to hear. They'd started speeding down the road, even faster than before.

"Can I at least say goodbye?"

Again, she didn't answer. Eden raised her voice. "CAN I SAY GOODBYE?"

"*No,*" Sylvana said sharply. She took a breath and smiled. "I mean, what's the point? It'll just complicate things." She nestled tiny white earphones in her ears and tapped the screen of her cell phone.

"We'll be there in thirty minutes," she said to someone on the phone. "Have everything ready."

The cell phone was lying on the car's center console. As Sylvana spoke, Eden looked down at it. On the screen was a photo of a dark-haired woman—presumably, the person she was speaking to. Beneath the photo was a single letter: *V.*

Something twisted in Eden's stomach.

The woman in the photo was the same V who'd approached her on the beach. The one who'd wanted to buy her bracelet and the lamp.

"Violet, I don't *care*," Sylvana said as she veered wildly around a car. "Whoever *wants* to fly it."

Violet. The name of another alum who'd been cut off from the lamp.

An unnerving revelation struck Eden like an electric shock:

V and Violet were one and the same.

She sat back in her seat. Now that she thought about it, the woman at the beach *had* looked a little too radiant to be mortal. If those big sunglasses hadn't covered Violet's eyes, maybe Eden would have recognized her.

Eden picked up the phone to see the photo more closely. As she did, something on the back of the gold-plated case caught her eye. Engraved across it was a word: ELECTRA.

The same word that was on Violet's business card.

Sylvana hadn't noticed that the phone was in Eden's hand. Carefully, she returned it to its place on the center console.

She'd been having so much fun for the past couple

hours that she'd forgotten how strange it was that Sylvana had shown up at school. Suddenly, it all seemed pretty bizarre. She'd known exactly where Eden was, and what to say to get her away.

Eden had seen Violet when Sasha's ankle was hurt at the beach. In fact, she'd hung around pretty closely. Could she have heard Eden telling the Rockwells she was from Sweden? Or that her mother was coming into town?

Suddenly she remembered that Tyler had thought someone was following them home—and then they'd all heard the beep outside the living room window.

Had Violet followed them?

Eden's heart was pounding. The pieces were coming together quickly—and forming a picture she didn't want to be true.

If Violet was an alum, that meant she knew about the bracelet's power. She'd know what would happen to Xavier and Goldie if it were removed. What's more, she'd know that if it were to come off, the lamp and its power would be up for grabs.

And if Violet was working with Sylvana...that meant Sylvana was after the same thing.

Eden shook her head. It seemed impossible. Sylvana was just like Eden! Anyway, she hadn't said a word about removing the bracelet.

But would that come later, once they were halfway across the world?

"Look, I've got to go." Ending her conversation, Sylvana tapped the phone's screen and removed the earphones.

Eden swallowed. If Sylvana's intentions were evil, she needed to know now. And she could only think of one way to find out.

"Let's not go back to school," she blurted out. "I don't ever want to see that lamp again."

Sylvana glanced at her. "But we're almost there."

"Do we have to? I just want to get to Paris."

Sylvana was silent for a moment, and Eden thought she might agree. With everything in her, she hoped she would. She wanted so badly to be wrong.

But then:

"Have you granted any wishes since you've been on Earth?"

"Just one." Eden's mind raced, wondering where the conversation would lead. "Yesterday I met a brother and sister. I thought the girl was going to die, so I panicked and told the brother to make a wish to save her life."

Sylvana tapped her fingers on the steering wheel. "So you're in the middle of a granting."

"Technically. But they don't know I'm a genie. And the second wish he tried to make was ungrantable, so they think the first one was a fluke. They don't know they have two more."

Sylvana pressed the gas a little harder. "At some point, that boy is going to say he wishes for *something*. Whether he intends to or not, he'll use those wishes. And when he does, you'll be sent back to the lamp."

The traffic light in front of them turned red precisely as they pulled beside a police car. Sylvana slammed on the brakes so violently, Eden's seat belt cut into her collarbone.

"Smile," Sylvana instructed as she beamed at the officers. Eden watched her in awe. To someone who didn't know better, she'd look positively angelic.

Sylvana turned to Eden. "What if I told you I can guarantee you'll never have to go back? Never have to grant another wish. You'll have total freedom on Earth, forever."

Eden started to feel light-headed.

"Because you don't have it yet, do you? You're here, but you still belong to the lamp. You're still at a wisher's mercy."

Sylvana reached across the console and slid a finger under the gold cuff around Eden's wrist. "All you have to do is take this off."

Eden shivered. Sylvana's touch was as soft as a feather.

"My bracelet?"

"Bracelet? More like a shackle. You'll never be free while you're wearing this thing." Sylvana's voice was low, and her eyes were entrancingly bright. "I took mine off, see?" She held up her bare right wrist. "To break my ties with the lamp forever."

Eden sat frozen, unable to speak.

"Do you know how to do it? I can tell you, if you like." She smiled disarmingly. "It's easy. Doesn't hurt."

The light turned green, and Sylvana sped off, blowing a kiss to the cops.

Watching her, Eden felt like she might cry.

"Having that thing off has made my life a whole lot better," Sylvana shouted over the wind. "Now they can't even send me those stupid messages!" She accelerated to pass another car. "Once it's off, you'll be just like me. Free as a bird! Isn't that what you want?"

Eden swallowed. "But . . . if I take off the bracelet, the lamp's enchantment will be broken," she said. "I wouldn't get my thousandth wish."

Sylvana shrugged. "If you stay here on Earth the way you want to, you're not going to get it anyway. Plus, if you come to Paris with me, I'll make sure you never need it."

"But what about Xavier and Goldie? Wouldn't it kill them?"

"What does it matter? You escaped! You don't want to go back. They're dead to you already."

Eden's light-headed feeling had swelled into a dizzying sense of disappointment. How could she have been so wrong about her hero?

"So what do you think?" Sylvana purred. "Does that sound like a plan?"

"Sure," Eden said flatly. "Once we're in Paris."

"Once we're in Paris." Sylvana couldn't hide her delight. "Gosh, it's going to be great." She stepped on the gas, and her hair flew behind her like a cloud of pure spun gold.

Seventeen

The convertible squealed to a stop in front of Mission Beach Middle.

"Make it quick." Sylvana pushed up her sunglasses. "The sooner we get to the airport, the better."

As Eden jogged away, she took a final glance back. Sylvana was already on her phone. Probably telling Violet, or someone else in her organization, that the lamp would soon be theirs.

Before long, she'd find out she was mistaken.

She should have known that the genie who was smart enough to escape the lamp was too smart to fall into her trap.

Eden picked up her speed and sprinted through the front doors. The truth about Sylvana had shot adrenaline through her veins. Nothing in the world could slow her down.

Just inside, Mr. Willis was standing by the office with his feet planted wide.

"Sweden! You're back!"

"My mom wants to talk to you!" Eden said as she whizzed by. "She's outside in the red car!"

At her locker, she fumbled with the combination lock. It took three tries before she got it right. At the very instant it popped open, the bell rang to end the school day.

Students swarmed the hall as she removed the borrowed denim backpack. She unzipped it a tiny bit— just enough to peek in at the lamp. Along with it was a brand-new parchment paper message. But there was no time to think about that now. Quickly, she zipped it back up and closed the locker.

When she looked up, Sasha and Tyler were coming toward her.

"Sasha! Tyler!" She was elated to see them. But it didn't look like they shared the sentiment.

"We need to talk to you," Tyler said sharply.

"Me too! I need your help!"

"First, maybe you can explain this." Sasha held up her phone.

On the screen was a text message:

Eden's not who you think she is. Ask her why she doesn't want you making any more wishes.

A ripple of anxiety ran through Eden. "Who sent you that?"

"We were hoping you could tell us," Sasha snapped.

"I don't know!"

"But is it true?" Tyler demanded. "Is there something you aren't telling us?"

Eden bit her lip. As she tried to think of the best way to respond, Bola rounded the corner.

Eden took a deep breath, trying to stay calm. "Look," she said. "I promise I'll explain everything. But first, I need help getting out of here. Fast. And—not through the front door."

The boys in orange jerseys from lunch barreled noisily down the hall, whooping and yelling. One even roared.

"Haven't we helped you enough already?" Sasha raised her voice to be heard over them.

"Eden!" Bola had spotted her through the madness. She started coming toward them fast, pushing kids aside to get through. She seemed to have grown even taller and more powerful during the day. Eden half expected her to breathe fire.

"Please?" Eden begged, feeling desperate.

Tyler had seen Bola too. He set his jaw. "Follow me." He grabbed Eden's hand and pulled her in the same direction as the football players.

"Tyler!" Sasha protested.

"Come *on*, Sash," he said. Then, to Eden: "Don't let go."

"I need to speak to you!" came Bola's voice from behind them.

The three of them darted into the thick of the crowd. Football players jostled and elbowed Eden as the horde carried them along. But she didn't dare let go of Tyler's hand, or even look back in Bola's direction. She understood what he was doing. The orange jerseys were serving as a moving shield around them.

They exited the building through a back door that opened to a parking lot. A long, dingy yellow bus was parked there, stretching across several spaces. Keeping as close to the center of the mob as possible, Eden and the Rockwells hustled across the pavement and onto the bus.

Tyler led them down the narrow aisle, past rows of well-worn black leather seats quickly filling with boys, to the very back. "Stay low and keep quiet," he murmured. "If we're lucky, they won't even notice we're here."

While Sasha slouched and sulked in the back corner, Eden and Tyler crouched on their knees and peeked through the back window. As the bus filled, the football team's chants and cheers escalated. So far, it seemed, they were successful stowaways.

"There she is," Eden whispered as Bola stormed out

of the school. She jogged around the parking lot, searching frantically. Finally, she went to a sleek black sedan about fifty yards behind the bus.

As she did, four women got out of the car. Eden gasped when she saw who they were.

Emerging from the driver's seat was Noel, the tough-looking genie who'd enabled Columbus to reach America.

From the passenger side came Ivy. Her silver-blond hair and pale skin were unmistakable. She was just as ethereal-looking on Earth as in the course guide.

Tabitha and Nala came out from the backseat. Naturally, Nala looked just as she had in the message from Capri. And Tabitha was no less blond or bodacious in real life.

Bola threw her hands in the air as she approached. She spoke with big hand gestures, presumably explaining how Eden had eluded her. Tabitha gave her a consoling hug, but the others stood around with their arms crossed.

Bola turned toward the bus, and Eden could swear she looked directly at them. She dropped flat on the seat. Her heart was pounding; she was sure she'd been caught. But just in time, the engine came to a shuddering start, and the bus rolled reluctantly forward. Stealing one more peek through the window, Eden saw that Bola's attention had returned to the other alumni.

As they rumbled out of the parking lot, she and Tyler sat up.

"Gosh, that was close." Eden sighed. "Thank you."

Sasha glared at her. "Are you ready to give us some answers?"

Eden glanced at the mass of orange jerseys in front of them. "Yeah. But not here."

"Well, then *where*?" Sasha was thoroughly annoyed.

"Should we go to the scrimmage?" Tyler asked. "It's at another school, farther inland."

"No, they might look there." Eden faced him. "You saw those women getting out of the car. Can you think of somewhere women like that would never go?"

He nodded slowly. "I've got an idea."

"This better be good," Sasha grumbled. "I'm going to miss volleyball practice."

"Now the question is, how do we get off this bus?"

But that problem, at least, solved itself. A football player's big red face appeared in front of them. "Hey! You're not on the team!" he shouted.

"You're right!" Eden said, smiling sweetly. "My bad. Now, would you mind dropping us off?"

The place Tyler had in mind was on the way to Mt. Carmel, so the bus driver agreed to drop them there. Tyler called it a skate park, but Eden couldn't understand why. The only green in sight was in the fronds of the palm trees that lined it.

It was a large structure, made entirely of concrete, with high sides that dropped to form a bowl-shaped hollow. At several points within the bowl, the concrete rose to form elevated flat-topped islands. Guys and girls ranging from elementary school age to adults swooped up and down the sides on boards like the ones in Tyler's half of the bedroom. Tyler, Sasha, and Eden sat cross-legged a few feet behind one of the ledges. And as the skateboarders dipped and rose, Eden turned the Rockwells' world upside down.

"You're a *genie*?!" Sasha burst out. It was maybe the third time she'd said it. The news seemed to be sinking in slowly.

"Let me get this straight. You're telling us that most of your life you've been miniature?" Tyler raised an eyebrow.

"Small as a bug!" Sasha marveled.

"Living in an *oil lamp*?"

"With your little parents!" Sasha added.

"They're *not* my parents." Eden supposed it was a lot for mortals to take in. "They're the masters of the lamp."

"So when I met you yesterday, where had you really come from?" Sasha asked.

"Under the sand, where the lamp was buried."

"You're *serious*?" she squealed. "*That's* why you were buried up to your face!"

"It definitely wasn't by choice," Eden said.

"Can I see the lamp again?" Tyler asked. Eden pulled it out of the backpack, and they stared in astonishment. "You *lived* in there?"

Sasha took it from her and put the spout to one eye. "Can they see me when I do this?"

"Actually, yes. Let's put it away." Hastily she shoved it back in the backpack.

"I think it's incredible," Sasha declared. "You get to live in this awesome little home and travel the world. And you get to *help* people. They must *love* you." She sighed. "You've got the best job in the universe. And you didn't even have to go to college."

"Honestly," Eden said, "you're making it sound way cooler than it is. I'm stuck in there *all the time*." She paused for emphasis, but they didn't seem to get it. "And when I go places for grantings, I'm there for such a short time—sometimes only a few minutes."

"But at least you get to *go*," Sasha said.

"How many countries have you been to?" Tyler asked.

"This is the twelfth."

He whistled, then drummed his fingers on his knee. "So you don't normally see the sun."

"Nope."

"Or the ocean."

"That's why you don't know how to swim!" Sasha said.

"Exactly."

"And no people except your parents," Tyler said.

"They're not—"

"Your *masters*. Sorry. Wait." He squinted at her. "Does this mean you're, like, a thousand years old?"

"*No!*" Eden said, horrified. "I'm twelve and a half!"

"Okay, good. That would be weird."

"No sun, no beach, no interaction with people your age. When you put it that way, it does sound sort of depressing," Sasha admitted.

"Why do you think I escaped?"

She examined Eden. "I guess you've never been to school before?"

"Nope."

"Well, that explains a lot." She and Tyler looked at each other and started cracking up.

"Was it that obvious?" Eden cringed.

"I guess you've done pretty well, considering," Tyler said, laughing. "But, yeah . . . we were starting to wonder if 'Swedish' was code for 'alien.'"

"I have a question," Sasha said, growing serious. "You told Tyler to wish to heal my ankle because you knew that if he did, you could grant it, right? But then you didn't grant his wish last night. Did you just... decide not to?"

"*No,*" Eden said quickly. "I wouldn't do that." She remembered the look on Tyler's face, and felt an uncomfortable pang of empathy. She shook her head. "Anyway, I can't choose whether to grant a wish. That one didn't work because of the rules."

"There are rules?"

Eden recited them. "The second rule blocked that wish," she said carefully.

They fell silent. The only sound was of skateboard wheels rolling against the concrete.

"We still don't know who sent me that message." Sasha rested her chin on her hand, thinking. "But whoever it was, they must want you to go back inside the lamp."

"I have a pretty good idea of who it might be." Eden explained what had really happened with Bola during World History. From there, she told them about Violet, Electra, the bracelet, and her afternoon with Sylvana.

"I *knew* there was something strange about Ms. Bola!" Sasha shook her head. "She was no normal teacher."

"And *I* knew I heard someone following us yesterday," Tyler said triumphantly. He smacked Sasha's arm. "See?"

"So there are two factions of genie alumni after you," Sasha said. "And each side wants something different, but neither of those is what *you* want."

"Basically," Eden said dismally. She'd broken it down quite well.

Sasha pulled out her phone to look at the text message again. "But how could Bola have messaged me?" she wondered. "Why would she have my number?"

"Who knows?" Eden said. "These alumni are tricky."

"Crap!" Sasha's eyes got big as she noticed something on her phone. She jumped up and brushed off her shorts. "I'm going to be late!"

"For what? You already missed practice," Tyler said.

"I'm babysitting at five!"

"Sash, this is important. Can't you call them and cancel?"

"Not on my first day! I don't want to lose this job."

"Well, be careful."

Sasha rolled her eyes.

"I'm serious. Don't talk to strangers."

"Especially beautiful women wearing gold cuff bracelets," Eden added.

"Right, right. Okay. I'll see you guys later, at home." The softening afternoon light framed Sasha's silhouette as she left.

"See this guy?" Tyler pointed out a tall teenager with a buzz cut. "He's really good." The guy jumped above his board, and it spun quickly beneath his sneakers in a full revolution before they hit it again.

"Can you do that?" Eden asked.

"A three-sixty flip? I wish."

"Hey, be careful with that word."

"Shoot, that's right." He gave her that crooked-tooth smile she was starting to know so well. "So as long as I follow those rules you told us, I really do get two more wishes?"

"Yeah." Eden's heart was heavy. She'd fought so hard to stay on Earth, but now he was sure to use the wishes in no time. Returning to the lamp was certainly a better option than sacrificing her masters' lives . . . but she was going to miss this place—and these mortals.

"Once I make them . . . do you *have* to go back?"

"That's how it works. I won't have a choice."

He nodded thoughtfully, then shook his bangs off his forehead. "Hey, let's go somewhere."

"Where?"

"Are you up for an adventure?"

She grinned. "Always."

Eighteen

Tyler led her down a tree-lined path. Most of the mortals on it were jogging, wearing sneakers and sunglasses. Some of them ran behind dogs attached to leashes they held in their hands. Eden observed them as they passed, and told Tyler the breed of each. The varieties of plants and trees she saw were easy to identify too. She loved seeing things she'd learned about in the pages of textbooks. She could even smell and touch them if she liked.

"I have to ask," Tyler said. "Does being a genie automatically make you a genius?"

"It's just that we use more of the space in our brains. And I have a really, really good teacher."

"No kidding. You know *everything*."

"Not *everything*."

"What's the longest river in Asia?"

"The Yangtze."

"What's thirty-two times one hundred and forty-five?"

"Four thousand, six hundred and forty."

"What kind of bush is that?" He pointed at a plant with clusters of long, spiky green and brown leaves.

"A Mojave yucca," she answered. *"Yucca schidigera."*

Eyebrows raised, he nodded. "So how does it feel?"

"How does *what* feel?"

"To be the smartest person I've ever met."

She had to laugh.

"Possibly the smartest person in San Diego."

"Ooh! One second." She'd spotted her first California white oak, and she wanted to feel its bark. When she did, she found herself face-to-face with a fascinating creature.

"Hello!" she greeted it.

It turned its head this way and that. It was roughly the size of a shoe, and it clung to the tree trunk with four tiny claws. It twitched its furry tail.

"You're a squirrel!" She could have sworn it nodded. "I didn't know you'd be so charming!"

"Possibly the smartest," Tyler said from behind her, "and probably the weirdest."

Eden turned to him. "These things are wonderful!"

"I wonder if I was ever this excited about trees and squirrels."

"How could you not be? They're incredible!"

"Kind of like what we think about living in a lamp," Tyler said. "And traveling the world to grant wishes."

Eden supposed it was the same. Maybe whatever wasn't normal to you seemed amazing. Did that mean she'd daydream about being a genie if she'd been born a mortal?

No way, she thought. She could never get tired of Earth.

"I'd switch places with you in a second," she said as they walked.

"Me?" He shook his bangs off his forehead. "I'm just an ordinary kid in California. There are millions of others like me. But *you*—you're one of a kind. Your whole life is magical."

"Your world is full of magic too," she said. "You'll never run out of places and things to explore!"

"I guess." Tyler shrugged. "If I can ever get to them. All I see is San Diego. I know it's beautiful, and I love living near the beach, but when you've been here your whole life, it gets kind of boring, you know?" He paused for a moment. "And I wouldn't mind trying somewhere new, to get away from bad memories here."

"What do you mean?"

"If you stick around long enough, you'll see. Sure, the world is amazing, but most of us are stuck with what we've got. Life can be really hard, you know? People hurt each other, lie, take advantage of each other. Bad things happen when you aren't expecting them."

What he was saying sounded a lot like Xavier's warnings. But just when she was about to argue—

"Duck," he said.

"Huh?"

He put his arm around her shoulder and pulled her to the ground.

"What—"

"Ssshhhh." He put his finger to his lips, then pointed through the bush in front of them. The sleek black car from the school parking lot was driving by very slowly. Eden held her breath. The windows were rolled down. Bola was leaning out of the back, scanning this way and that like a sentry on watch. In the seat beside her were Tabitha and Nala. Noel was driving, and Ivy sat in the passenger seat.

They were scoping the area. They'd probably comb the whole city for her.

Eden and Tyler stayed down for a while after the car had passed. When she finally looked away from the street, he was staring at her.

"This is serious," he said.

She shrugged uncomfortably.

"You really don't want to go back, do you?" Tyler asked.

"Well . . . no."

A man jogging by with headphones in his ears almost ran into them, then nearly lost his balance as he veered away. He turned back and glared.

Tyler held out a hand to Eden. "We should be clear. I bet they won't come back this way." She took it, and he helped her stand up. "We're almost there anyway," he said.

A few minutes later, they reached the mysterious structures she'd seen looming in Mission Beach's backdrop, including the roller coaster.

"Here we are!" he announced.

She blinked. "We're going *here*?"

"You wanted an adventure, right?"

The park was even stranger and more amazing than she could have imagined. She sprinted from one mechanism to another. On one of them, four mortals strapped themselves into seats and were lifted a hundred feet for a high-speed drop to the ground. Another had cups spinning wildly on a platform while the platform itself spun and tilted. And of course, there was the sprawling centerpiece: the roller coaster.

Each mechanism was more dazzling than the last. But it was odd. Mortals were smiling when they stepped out of the little cars or the attendants unstrapped them from their seats. By all appearances, they were elated.

But while they were on the mechanisms, their screams rose and fell like ocean waves.

"Why do they do it?" Eden asked Tyler. They'd come to a stop in front of a foreboding structure a sign identified as the Octotron.

"Do what?"

"Put themselves on the mechanisms. If they're afraid, why do they do it?"

"Mechanisms?" Tyler tossed his bangs out of his eyes. "You mean rides."

"Rides," Eden said. It seemed like a strange word for them. "They seem afraid. Why do they get on?"

Tyler thought about that for a minute. "For a thrill, I guess," he said. "They have safety belts and brakes. They're not really scared."

"But if they didn't have safety belts and brakes, they could die."

"That's probably true," he said. "So where should we start?"

It was on the first drop of the roller coaster that Eden understood. The car's creaky climb had brought them higher and higher above the pavement, the sand, and the vast rippling ocean. But as it tipped over the edge, she felt the rush of wind in her face and her heart soared. She screamed her head off just like a mortal.

As they plummeted down one of the drops, Eden

took her hands off the rail and raised them in the air. "Smile!" Tyler yelled as a light flashed in front of them.

When they got off, he showed her what the flash had been: a camera. A station showed images of the roller coaster cars, captured as they whizzed by. Theirs showed their hands in the air and pure bliss on their faces. Freedom, Eden thought. Tyler bought two copies and gave one to Eden.

Next they tried the Vertical Plunge. On this one, a harness strapped their torsos in, but their legs swung free. As the seat rose, the mortals below them grew smaller and smaller, until they looked no bigger than ants. Finally Tyler and Eden stopped at the top and lingered for a painstaking moment. At the very instant when the suspense became too much to bear, they dropped. The sensation was unreal.

After that they rode the bumper cars, which was almost—but not quite—as turbulent as riding in Sylvana's convertible. Gleefully they crashed and collided with other mortals' cars.

But the roller coaster was Eden's favorite. They rode it three more times, and each was better than the last. When they stepped off after the fourth time, she wondered if the feeling of motion would ever leave her. She sort of hoped it wouldn't.

She couldn't stop smiling as they strolled down the path.

"I have a question," Tyler said.

"Go ahead."

He cleared his throat. "These other two *things* I have. You know what I mean. I don't want to say it."

She swallowed. "Yeah, I know."

"I was thinking. What if I used one to ask if you can stay here forever?"

It felt like a thousand seeds planted inside her brain were growing and blossoming into flowers all at once. She thought she might faint with happiness.

"What do you think?" he said. "Can we do it?"

How badly she wanted to say yes! But the truth tugged at her like an anchor. "I don't think so," she said reluctantly. "I'm bound to the lamp."

Disappointment darkened his face—but he wasn't quite ready to give up yet. "Can't we try?"

What was the worst that could happen? She'd had wishes denied before. And even though her head knew it was impossible, in her heart was a shimmer of hope.

She took a breath. "Go ahead," she said. "But word it carefully. Wish for forever."

A scream whipped past them as a roller coaster car zoomed by. He took a step toward her. Amidst the roaring rides, they were the park's still, quiet nucleus.

Her heart pounded as he drew close.

"I wish Eden could stay on Earth forever. No longer a genie, but a regular girl."

The sound of his words made her shiver. For one delicious, drawn-out moment more she savored the sweet possibility.

But then she knew she couldn't do it.

She yearned to snap her fingers and grant the wish that would set her free. But granting wishes was what she knew best, and as soon as Tyler said it she knew for sure it was ungrantable.

In order for a wish to be granted, the wisher, the genie, and the lamp had to be in accord. On this one, Eden and Tyler were alone. The lamp wasn't going to budge.

Sadly, painfully, she shook her head.

"I keep striking out on these wishes." He studied the ground, then looked at her again. "But I don't want you to go back."

Her heart hummed with feeling. "You don't?"

"No." His eyes remained locked on hers. "So I'm not going to let it happen."

Eden had traveled to twelve countries. She'd lived like a princess, been pampered and indulged, and seen wonders most mortals would never see. But she'd never known anything as wonderful as the way those words made her feel.

"But how?" she asked him.

"We'll hide you."

"Where?"

"With us. I'll tell Dad...um..." He thought for a moment. "I know. I'll tell him you're a foreign exchange student, and you need a host home. He won't mind."

"But your wishes. Don't you want them?"

He shook his head. "Eventually I'll make the second one. It'll be the world's greatest wish. It's got to be, because it'll be my last."

Euphoria was pumping through her veins. "You're sure?"

"Yes."

"There's something else, though. If the Loyals see I really won't make the request for reentry, they may try to pressure you into making the other wishes."

"They'll only be wasting their time," he said. "You're not going anywhere." He held up a closed fist with the last finger extended. "I pinky swear," he said. He took her hand, folded her fingers the same way, and entwined her pinky with his own. Then he kissed where his thumb met his forefinger, and nodded for her to do the same.

"Pinky swear," said Eden, feeling dizzy.

"But for now"—he smiled—"one more time on the roller coaster?"

She grinned. *"Yes."*

As long as she was here, she'd ride it as many times as she could.

Nineteen

That night at a quiet bistro in downtown San Diego, nine disgruntled genie alumni convened around a back table.

They were finishing a decadent meal. There had been fresh oysters to start, then entrées ranging from lamb to lobster. Bola had ordered the catch of the day, a local halibut served with capers and cauliflower mash. Several bottles of expensive wine sat in ice buckets next to the table.

The restaurant's décor reminded Bola of the lamp's interior, which was, perhaps, why she liked it so much. The lighting was dim, with candles on each table, and the maroon wallpaper was patterned with gold.

Tonight was the first time in history that so many loyal alumni had gathered in one place—and yet, the mood was far from celebratory. Circumstances were dire.

In addition to the Loyals who'd been at the school in the afternoon, three others had joined them. Cadence, who'd preceded Eden as resident genie, had come from her villa in Spain. Alessandra had flown in from Moscow. And Scarlett, who preferred a simple life, had driven a station wagon from her ranch in Iowa.

Of course, the alum who looked most out of place at the table was Genevieve. Having wished to spend forever in a twelve-year-old girl's body, she often got strange looks when she was with the others. But in this case, her unusual final wish had made her invaluable.

"Who else is coming to San Diego?" Alessandra asked.

"Bianca and Karla arrive tomorrow morning," Bola said.

"What about Barbara Jean?" Scarlett asked.

Bola scowled.

"She's Electric," Noel snapped.

"No way! When did she cross over?"

"At least a hundred years ago." Noel shot Scarlett a look that Bola was sure had struck many a chord in the courtroom. "You'd be wise to try to stay up-to-date on matters of the lamp."

"*Sorry.*" Scarlett scowled.

"It *is* hard to keep up these days," said Tabitha. Of all the Loyals, she was the nicest—always trying to smooth things over. After more than two thousand years on Earth, *nice* wasn't Bola's priority. Especially tonight. They were here to save the lamp.

"How many of ... *them* ... do we think are here?" Cadence asked haltingly. As the youngest alum, she regarded Bola with reverence—and, perhaps, a touch of fear.

"Sylvana, obviously," said Bola. "Genevieve was in the classroom with Eden when she checked her out of school. It sounds like she claimed she was her mother." Genevieve nodded.

"If she's here, surely there are others," Nala said. "She's got them all at her beck and call."

Indeed, Sylvana had amassed a disconcerting number of alumni over the past 250 years. She'd formed Electra in 1757. Among mortals, it was known as one of Earth's top auction houses, along with the likes of Sotheby's and Christie's. However, the alumni around the table knew that its operations were essentially a front for its true goal: to procure the lamp—and, more importantly, its powers.

Centuries earlier, when rumors had first swirled that Sylvana was on a mission to seize the lamp, most alumni had laughed it off. Even for her, the world was big. Eager mortals made their wishes in a flash, so the lamp generally disappeared soon after it was found. For her to get her hands on it would be nearly impossible.

But then she'd started acquiring associates, who

came to be known as the Electric. The first to go was Athena, the very first genie who'd resided in the lamp. Next was Violet. Then Kingsley, Monroe, and many others. All in all, fifteen that Bola knew of—about half the alumni on Earth. Sylvana's contingent had become a force to be reckoned with.

"My guess is she's got as many of them in town as possible," Tabitha said, biting the last bit of meat off a chicken bone. "After all, she *is* their boss. They have to do what she says."

"And as we all know, Sylvana's power of persuasion is formidable," Bola said.

"But Eden didn't leave with her today. She came back," Ivy pointed out. Her gentle voice was reassuring to them all. "And Xavier and Goldie are still alive and well. If she'd fallen for Sylvana's charms, she would have taken off the bracelet already."

"She's alarmingly headstrong." Bola shook her head, thinking of their exchange. The girl's audacity had shocked her.

"But she *is* vulnerable," Genevieve said. Besides Bola, she was the only one who'd interacted with Eden so far. "She doesn't fit in with the other kids—and I made sure she knows it."

"Did you tell her friend she was withholding information?" Noel asked.

"Yeah, I sent a text message to the girl she's staying

with. Got the number from one of her two-faced little friends." She shrugged. "No response. The last they were seen, at the end of school, they were together. That's when they slipped away from Bola." Bola stiffened at the memory. She still couldn't believe she'd let it happen.

"We have to remember," Ivy said, "Xavier and Goldie say she knows right from wrong."

"Right from wrong," Nala mused. "That's what this is, isn't it? Us versus them. And it's up to her to choose."

"I don't think we need to worry," Ivy said. "She understands what's at stake. The masters say she won't give up the bracelet."

"Even when Sylvana ups the pressure?" Nala argued. "*I* wouldn't want to be in that position."

"The fact is, as long as she's on Earth, we have a major problem on our hands," Bola said.

"And yet, she refuses to return to the lamp," Nala said. "So how do we change her mind?"

The table fell silent as waiters came to clear it. Across from Bola, Cadence perused the dessert menu discreetly. Tabitha showed photos on her phone to Alessandra, giggling quietly. The others sipped their water or what was left in their wineglasses. They were a listless bunch.

Bola felt a surge of frustration. These were *genies*! They'd granted wishes that had helped shape Earth's history. Every one of them was graceful, brilliant, and terribly beautiful. Nothing in the mortal world could compare to the greatness they were born into.

So why were they sitting in a San Diego restaurant with the spirit of a defeated army?

"Would you like dessert?" the waiter asked.

"Yes," said Bola, filled with new resolve. "Espressos all around. And one of everything on the dessert menu, for the table."

Nodding, the waiter whisked away. The alumni awaited Bola's next words expectantly.

"Ladies," she declared, "we cannot stand for this. We will not give up. We will not surrender. And we will not leave this table until we have a solution." She squared her shoulders. "Tomorrow, we are going to save our lamp."

Twenty

"There you are!" Sasha said when Eden and Tyler got home. She and Mr. Rockwell were on the sofa, watching TV.

Eden looked at the clock. It was 9 P.M. The past few hours had slipped away.

"Sorry!" she said, blushing. She still had that magic feeling from the amusement park. When she walked, it felt like her feet didn't touch the ground.

"I just got home too," Sasha said. "Dad had a couple visitors while we were gone." She raised her eyebrows meaningfully.

Eden's breath caught in her throat like water swallowed the wrong way.

"Yes, your mother and your aunt stopped by." There was a dreamy, faraway look in Mr. Rockwell's eyes. "Lovely people."

"My mother and my aunt." It must have been Sylvana and—who? Violet? "What did they say?"

"They were looking for you."

"Weird." Eden tried to act nonchalant.

"I told them you never came home from school. They said you were supposed to leave with them today."

"I wasn't— They must have been confused." She smiled tightly. "Language barrier."

"Well, they said you'll have to leave tomorrow instead."

"Eden's actually going to stay here for a while," Tyler said. "That's okay, right, Dad?"

Sasha's eyebrows shot up.

"Oh, sure," Mr. Rockwell said absently. "As long as it's fine with her mother."

"I'll make sure she understands," Eden assured him.

"There was one more thing she said to tell you. What was it?" Mr. Rockwell scratched his head. "Oh, right. They said not to worry, because they'll find you."

"Well that's a relief," Tyler said sarcastically.

Eden shook her head and smiled halfheartedly. "Trust me, that is one thing I'm not worried about."

Before long, Mr. Rockwell said he was going to bed. Eden excused herself too, leaving Tyler and Sasha in the living room. In the bathroom, she unbraided her hair and brushed it until it rippled with soft waves. She splashed water on her face and washed her hands. Then she went to Sasha's room, sat on the air mattress, and unzipped the backpack.

Ever since she'd seen there was a new message from the lamp, it had lingered in the back of her mind. She supposed that if she'd been able to finish watching the message at the beach, Xavier and Goldie might have told her who "V" really was—and warned her to steer clear of Sylvana. It probably wouldn't be a bad idea to see what they had to say now.

Carefully she unrolled the parchment paper, and her masters' faces appeared. They were even more bedraggled than before. The circles under Xavier's eyes had grown darker, and Goldie was paler and thinner than Eden had ever seen her. They were probably taking turns keeping vigil at the telescope. Seeing the state they were in, Eden wondered if they'd even eaten or slept.

Xavier rubbed his temples wearily. "I hope you'll watch this one," he said.

"Dear, we're not trying to ruin your fun," Goldie said. "We only want what's best for you."

Guilt tugged at Eden's conscience. She'd never seen them look so defeated.

"Bola told us that Sylvana checked you out of school today," said Goldie. "By the time you receive this message—well, we may already be gone." Eden realized they would have recorded this while she was with Sylvana and the lamp was back in her locker. That meant they couldn't see anything through the telescope. She'd literally left them in the dark, thinking any moment could be their last.

"If you're seeing this, and you haven't removed the bracelet yet," Xavier said, "I implore you—please do not. Not just for us, but for yourself, the lamp, and the world. By now, we expect you know that Sylvana is trying to seize the lamp and its power for herself. If she were to get what she wants . . ." He shook his head, at a loss for words.

"We created the lamp for good," Goldie said earnestly. "We used to be mortal, you know—thousands of years ago. We've lived on Earth, and seen terrible darkness. When the opportunity arose to enchant the lamp, we decided to make it something to give mortals a reason to hope, and dream, and wonder."

"*That's* the lamp's true power," Xavier said. "Not just granting wishes, but giving hope. We designed the system so that very few mortals would ever find the lamp. It was essential to us that a visit from a genie should never be commonplace. In fact, it should be the sort of thing mortals would tell stories about, and those who heard them would wonder if those stories could be true."

"If that glimmer of hope existed, that maybe the world does contain *real* magic," Goldie said, "we thought maybe that would give some mortal, at some point, a reason to keep carrying on."

Xavier nodded and wrapped his arm around Goldie. "That's what we intended," he said. "But Sylvana's intentions are nothing like ours."

"She's ravenous for power!" Goldie said fiercely. "She was always twisting mortals' wishes to hurt them. She would have taken off her own bracelet just to spite us, except she knew it would cost her her final wish."

"If she gets what she wants," Xavier continued, "she'll have unlimited power to do whatever harm she likes to Earth and the mortals on it. Can you imagine?"

"We told you there's never been a genie like you," Goldie said. "And that's the truth! No matter what you think, you're not like her. You never have been. Eden, you were born to be a genie. And you're a *good* genie. Look at your bracelet and *remember*!"

"We're begging you," Xavier implored. "Come home. Here is where you're meant to be."

Goldie blew her a kiss, and the message ended.

Eden let the parchment paper roll back up and laid it next to her on the air mattress. Ignoring Xavier and Goldie's pleas was more difficult when she could see the sad state they were in.

Why hadn't they told her the truth about Sylvana before? She supposed they'd wanted to keep her safe and innocent. They must have thought they were doing the right thing. But then, they'd never really known what was right for her.

Still, she couldn't let them go on thinking she might pull the plug at any moment. She sighed in submission. It was time to check in.

"I can't believe I'm doing this," she murmured. She swiped a hand across the paper to clear her masters' message.

"Hi," she said to the paper. "It's me. I guess you know I haven't taken off the bracelet." She held it up to show them. "I'm safe, and so are you.

"Look ... I just watched your message. Why didn't you tell me all that before?" She felt herself growing annoyed, then remembered they'd spent all day fearing for their lives, and held it off. "I know all about Electra. Sylvana and Violet have both tried to get me to take off my bracelet. But I know better!" She ran a hand through her braid-crimped hair. "I'm still mad at you guys. I mean, come on. You've been lying to me for my entire life. But I'd never do that to you."

She cleared her throat. "I know you want me to come back. Bola and some of the other Loyal alumni have been trying to convince me too. But the truth is ... I don't want to." Her eyes fell on the photo of baby Sasha and Tyler with their mother. "I want to stay here, with these mortals. I know you don't trust mortals, but these are good ones." She thought about the wish Tyler had tried to make, and remembered what it felt like being next to him on the roller coaster. "I love it here."

She heard laughter from the living room. It was time to wrap things up.

"Look, I don't want you to worry. No matter what, you're safe. But when you say I was born to be a genie . . . I still don't know if I believe that. And I need to be here to find out."

Footsteps were coming down the hall.

"*Don't worry,*" she repeated emphatically. She rolled up the parchment to end the message.

The door clicked open.

"What are you doing?" Sasha asked.

"Want to see something cool?" Eden touched the rolled-up parchment to the lamp's spout, and the lamp sucked it inside like an animal swallowing food.

"What in the *world*?" Sasha took a step back.

"Magic," Eden said with a smile.

Sasha sat on her bed. "Can you believe Sylvana came here?"

"Yeah, I can," Eden said. "She's ruthless."

Sasha shook her head. "I can't stop thinking about everything you told us. It's insane."

"I know."

Sasha bit her lip. "Ty just told me he's only going to make one more of those wishes. So you can stay on Earth."

Eden watched her, wondering how she felt about that. It was difficult to tell.

She shifted her weight on the air mattress. "I hope you don't mind," she said. "Me staying here, I mean. Since I've been here, you guys have given me...well, everything." The reality was that without them, she wouldn't have food, shelter, clothes—or friends. "I don't know what I would have done without you."

She watched Sasha think it over, tugging on her ponytail. "It's okay," she said finally. "I wish you didn't lie to us, of course. But you risked your freedom to help me at the beach when you barely even knew me. I don't know many people who would do that." She raised an eyebrow. "I mean, today my best friends ditched me because they met someone cooler. People can be brutal, you know?"

"Tell me about it."

Sasha smiled. "Anyway, we've got to keep you around long enough to make that other wish, right?"

"Right," Eden agreed.

"So what happens now?" Tyler asked, coming through the door. He stopped short. "Am I interrupting girl talk?"

"Nah, you're okay." Sasha patted the plaid bedspread beside her, and Tyler sat. "That's a good question. Eden, what's next? Are you going to go to school tomorrow?"

"Bola will still be there," Tyler pointed out.

"True," Eden said. "And other Loyals may be too."

"And what about Electra?" Sasha asked.

"I'd say there's a good chance they'll show up. Although I'm definitely not going to Paris with my 'mother,' that's for sure."

"At least at school you'd have a little bit of a buffer," Sasha offered. "Adults aren't allowed to just wander in."

"As long as Principal Willis holds his ground," Eden said. "You haven't met Sylvana. She's incredibly persuasive." She thought for a moment. "But you know what? I don't care. I came here to be free, like a mortal—I mean, like you guys. I'm not going to hide from them."

"Then that's that," Tyler said. "Day two, here we come."

Sasha peered at her curiously. "Eden, are you afraid?"

It was a fair question.

"A little," she admitted. "But not as much as I love the world."

Twenty-One

That night, strange dreams haunted Eden's sleep. In one of them, she was swimming in the sea. When she came up for air, Goldie was treading water beside her. But when Eden called out to her, she swam away so fast Eden couldn't catch her.

Then, in the next instant, she remembered that she didn't know how to swim.

In the morning, the sound of Sasha's alarm woke her. The sun was just starting to illuminate the sky. Eden showered and dressed in a tank top and shorts from Sasha's dresser.

She, Tyler, and Sasha sat around the kitchen table and ate toast. Although Mr. Rockwell had left for work before sunrise, they didn't say a word about genies or the lamp. Instead, they joked around about teachers and kids at school. It was a refreshing change. For a moment, Eden let herself pretend she was a real mortal, with no bigger cares than last night's homework.

After breakfast, she nestled the lamp and her notebook in the backpack. Together, the three of them set off for school.

Along the way, Eden kept a sharp lookout for the Loyals' black car and Sylvana's convertible. Thankfully, neither made an appearance. When at last they stepped into the lobby of Mission Beach Middle, she breathed a deep sigh of relief. So far, so good.

For an hour and a half after the first bell rang, nothing noteworthy happened at all. Tentatively, like a seedling in spring, Eden's hope began to grow. Maybe, just maybe, the alumni had given up.

On top of everything else, Gigi didn't answer to her name during first-period roll call. Swiveling around in her seat, Eden was pleased to see her desk was empty.

So far, things couldn't be going more smoothly.

But then, midway through Spanish, the fire alarm went off.

At first Eden didn't know what it was. Initially the school bell had frightened her, but now the sound of it was as normal as the chiming of Xavier's clocks. But this was different. Instead of a single long tone, it was a constant pulse at earsplitting volume.

The response from her classmates was different too.

They seemed to be looking for someone to show them how to react. Some seemed excited, but others were nervous and unsure.

Mr. Willis's voice piped through the speakers: "Ladies and gentlemen, vacate the building immediately through the back doors."

"You think it's a real fire?" someone asked behind her.

"No way. It's got to be a drill," another student answered.

"But why would they do it on the second day of school?"

"Class!" said Mrs. Cantrell. She ran a hand through her short salt-and-pepper hair. "You know what to do. Walk calmly in single file down the hall, then form a line outside. *Vamanos.*"

"Is it a real fire?" someone called.

Mrs. Cantrell shrugged. "How should I know?"

Sasha and Eden stuck close together. They didn't speak, but Eden suspected they were thinking the same thing: she'd be an easier target outside.

When they walked past a restroom, Sasha ducked in and pulled Eden behind her.

"We'll wait it out here," she said. "You'd be too exposed out there."

"Ladies." Emerging from a stall, Ms. Bola blotted magenta lipstick on a sheet of toilet paper and shot them a smile that made Eden's skin crawl. "*So* glad we ran into each other. But you hear the alarm. We've got to get out of here quickly. Safety first." She gripped their shoulders with hands like talons and pushed them out the door. Sasha and Eden eyed each other in terror, but there was nothing they could do.

Ms. Bola pushed Sasha into the stream of students pouring through. "Run along," she said. "Eden and I have business to attend to."

"I'm not leaving her!" Sasha cried.

"Principal," Ms. Bola said, seeing Mr. Willis standing guard. "Will you please escort Sasha Rockwell outside? She seems to be confused about fire alarm protocol."

Mr. Willis's eyes lit up. "Behavioral problems? Thanks, Bola." As he dragged Sasha away by the elbow, she looked back helplessly at Eden.

"*Behavioral problems?*" Ms. Bola said, mimicking him as she pushed Eden around the corner. "What an idiot."

"Did you pull that alarm?" Eden demanded.

"Of course I did. How else was I going to get you alone?"

Bola steered Eden into the gym. Their shoes squeaked as they crossed the shiny wooden floor with its mysterious patterns of lines and circles.

"Where are you taking me?"

"You'll see soon enough."

On the opposite end was an open doorway. A sign above it read, GIRLS.

"Through here," Bola said, and shoved her in.

A rank, faintly chemical smell hung in the air. As Bola led her across the faded tile, past dingy sea-green lockers and graffiti-covered toilet stalls, the smell grew stronger.

Finally they reached a door: another exit. They passed through it and stepped into a new room.

The sickly smell from the locker room was so thick, you could almost see it. There were no windows, and the air felt moist and heavy. It was like being in a cave.

Two long rectangular lights buzzed from the ceiling, shining dimly on a concrete floor that dipped down into a submerged pool of water.

Bola had led her to an indoor swimming pool. Eden hadn't even known there was one at the school.

As she took in her surroundings, Eden quickly realized things could—and would—get worse. Bola hadn't brought her there so they could be alone. Ten other women were waiting.

That is—nine women, and one girl. Among the Loyals was Gigi.

They faced her as she walked in. A few stood in front of the pool, while the others lined its perimeter. Each of them was uncommonly lovely, but no two looked the same.

Eden didn't need to see their bracelets to know she'd entered a room full of Loyal alumni.

Noel and Nala darted forward and grasped Eden's arms. She resisted, but they were stronger. They pulled her toward the pool. Suddenly someone pushed her from behind, and before she could think, she was falling forward. She closed her eyes and braced herself for the impact.

The front of her body slapped the water's surface like a pancake landing its flip.

"Belly flop!" someone hooted as she rose up, gasping for air. "That must've hurt!" A chorus of female giggles bounced off the walls.

Her heart was a tambourine, twisting percussively this way and that. She tried to collect her breath, but the humid air was like a cloth shoved deep in her throat. She moved her arms and legs madly, panicking, desperate to stay afloat.

After all, she still didn't know how to swim.

Her big toe scraped against something. Solid ground. She found it with the other foot. If she stood on the tips of her toes, her chin grazed the water's surface.

She reminded herself that she wasn't going to drown. That was one thing she had going for her.

The women had distributed themselves around the pool. With the exception of Gigi, she knew every face from the course guide. Until now, they'd been mythical heroines to her.

Taking in the sight of them, she slipped on a slick tile and swallowed a mouthful of dull aqua blue. The taste of chlorine was sharp in her mouth. With one foot in front of the other, she climbed the slippery inclined floor.

"Thank you for joining us," came Bola's voice. She'd climbed up to the high diving board, so she towered above them.

"You didn't give me a choice," Eden said. Her voice was small in the stifling room. A few genies laughed, and Bola shot them a glance that glittered with reproach. Even among her fellow alumni, her authority was unchallenged.

"I would argue that you didn't give *us* a choice," Bola countered. "First you disobeyed your masters, and then you defied me."

"And I'm going to keep on doing it," Eden said. Her body was pulsing with anger. "I'm staying here on Earth. I hope you know that throwing me in a pool isn't going to change that."

"This is bigger than you." Bola stepped forward on the diving board. "You were born to the lamp for a reason. You're not meant for this world."

"Maybe I am!" Eden shot back. She looked around the room. "None of you knows a thing about me. Since I've been here, all you've done is chase me and bully me." She pointed at Gigi. "Especially you! Why are you here, anyway? Did they convince you to help them?"

"They didn't have to." Gigi held up her wrist. On it was a gold cuff that her long-sleeved dress had concealed the day before. "I told you to go back where you came from."

"*You're* an alum? But you're my age!"

"I *look* like I am. I wished to be twelve years old forever. You probably know me as Genevieve."

Genevieve was resident genie from AD 657 to 740. Eden had never seen a message from her, but she could picture her portrait in the course guide: a pretty woman with thick hair and dimples. What Gigi would look like if she were an adult.

Eden shook her head. "You all have some serious issues."

Noel spoke up. "We're under strict orders from the lamp's masters—"

"You think I care about their orders?"

"We don't think you want them to die," Noel said gravely. "And if Electra receives the lamp, they will."

"Electra's not going to get the lamp!" Eden wrapped her arms around herself. She'd made her way to water that reached only midway up her rib cage, but she was soaked from head to toe. Her green cotton tank top clung wetly to her skin. "I'm not going to take off my bracelet! I just want to live on Earth."

"And you think Sylvana's going to allow that?" Bola demanded.

"You don't know what she's capable of," said Tabitha, more gently than the others. "She'll do *anything* to get the lamp's power. Things you can't even imagine."

"I held her off before," Eden said. "I'll do it again."

"You don't understand," Noel cut in.

"So we're going to have to make you," said Bola. "Ivy?"

Ivy was standing right next to the diving board. She nodded at Bola and snapped, and the dim lights extinguished completely. The pool was dark as midnight.

A shiver ran up Eden's spine. She'd forgotten that alumni could wish for magical powers as part of their last wishes. There was no telling what might come next.

Suddenly, she was outside—but not in San Diego, and not during the day. Above her was the endless night sky, adorned with no fewer stars than in the lesson room's maps of constellations. For so many of them to be visible, there must be no light pollution for hundreds of miles.

Beneath her, long grass waved in the breeze. The air was crisp, with a cool, pleasant bite. Nearby, several large mounds rose up from the land like grassy pyramids, with structures that looked like homes built on their flat tops.

As her eyes adjusted, Eden saw a group of people standing between two of the mounds. Their skin and hair were dark, and pieces of cloth hung from bands tied around their waists. Red makeup was painted on some of their faces in artful designs. There were men, women, and children—maybe thirty in all.

Eden crept toward them. They were gathered around a woman whose back was turned. She wore a long purple gown, and her hair was the color of honey.

As Eden rounded the side and stood behind the group of people, she saw the woman's face. It was Sylvana.

Out of the darkness came Bola's voice. "You're in North America, in part of what we now call Illinois. The year is 1320." Eden looked for Bola, but she didn't see her. And though her voice seemed to boom from the sky, it seemed that no one else could hear her—or, for that matter, see or hear Eden.

Based on the time and location, the mortals with Sylvana must be Mississippians. They were a Native American culture that Xavier had taught about in history lessons. The mounds currently surrounding Eden were the building blocks of their communities.

"This was one of Sylvana's many grantings that you didn't read about in the course guide," Bola continued. "In a moment, you'll understand why."

Eden studied Sylvana's face. She appeared younger than she'd chosen to look for immortality, but her eyes were unmistakable.

One man was standing in front of the others, speaking to her. He held the lamp reverently in his hands, which Eden assumed meant he must be the wisher. She couldn't hear their words, but she saw Sylvana lift her hand and snap her fingers. When she did, she vanished—which meant the man must have just made his third wish.

Suddenly a gust of wind cut through the air, so strong Eden almost lost her balance. Mothers tried to shield their children, and men and women clutched one another.

There was another blast of wind, even stronger this time. The long grass flapped madly. Eden had to drop to her knees; she could no longer stand on two legs.

High above, the swirling gales were taking on a recognizable shape. Eden stared in utter disbelief as she saw a funnel cloud form with alarmingly unnatural speed. Careening quickly toward them was a natural disaster that had long fascinated her in Xavier's science lessons: a tornado.

Its might was absolutely incomprehensible. As it

drew closer, Eden clutched the wildly waving grass beneath her, but the blades kept breaking off. A chorus of terrified screams rose up against the roar of the wind as the funnel cloud advanced. Several people tried to outrun it. One of them, a woman, screamed hysterically as it lifted her off the ground. Eden squeezed her eyes shut.

"Make it stop!" She could barely keep her grip on solid ground. The tornado was lifting her own legs, pulling them toward it. "Bola, please! Make it stop!"

And suddenly, it did.

She was on her hands and knees, panting. But she was no longer on the grass where the tornado had hit—and she wasn't back in the pool, either. Instead, she'd arrived somewhere entirely different.

"What you just saw was a typical wish granted by Sylvana," came Bola's voice. Her sharp British accent made the words cut like blades. "The man you saw wished for a change in weather. His village needed relief from the drought that was killing their crops. Rather than helping them, Sylvana granted his wish with an act of destruction."

Eden was speechless. Sure, she'd twisted a few wishes for fun—but going *this* far off course was inconceivable to her.

"Now, pay attention, Eden. The year is now 1348. You're in Florence, Italy."

It was daytime here. Beneath Eden was a dirt path. She heard a horse's hooves clop by behind her. Brushing her hands off, she stood up.

The street was deserted. There was an eerie stillness in the air.

And yet, not far away, strange sounds rose up like ghosts. They sounded like the voices of mortals, but Eden had never heard mortals make such horrible, desolate sounds before. Ignoring the pounding in her chest, she followed them.

Suddenly, a man staggered across her path.

"*Aiuto!!*" the man rasped as he darted by with jerky movements. "*Aiuto!!*"

"Help me," in Italian.

Eden continued forward in the direction the man had come from. Around the corner, she came upon a woman sitting on the ground, weeping softly. In her arms was a bundle of cloth that she cradled like a child.

"*Il mio bambino!*" she cried. "*Il mio bambino sta morendo!*" *My baby is dying.*

The moans were coming from others who lay prone on the ground, up and down the street. Eden's eyes flitted from one to another in horror. It was as if they were all waiting for their turn to die.

Her breathing had grown jagged and painful. She'd studied European history well enough to realize what she'd stepped into.

But could it really be the work of Sylvana? It seemed too terrible to be true.

"Several years before this, Sylvana granted a wish for a man in Asia. He wanted to make his mark on the world," boomed Bola's voice. "She made that man the first carrier of a disease that spread like wildfire and devastated Europe."

"The Black Death," Eden said. Her eyes were fixed on the woman holding the baby.

"More than seventy-five million people were killed," Bola said. "All because of a single wayward wish."

A rat ran right in front of Eden's toes, and she screamed and jumped back. It was like living in a nightmare. Suddenly, she couldn't take any more.

"Get me out of here!" she screamed into the sky. "I've seen enough!"

A set of hands gripped her arms.

"Enough!" she wailed, trying to shake them off.

But then she realized water was splashing as she writhed around. The strong hands locked around her lifted her easily out of the pool.

The dim lights were back on. The hands that had lifted Eden out belonged to two stern, unfamiliar men. They wore spotless black suits, and earpieces attached to curly plastic cords.

"Eden," one of them said, "you're coming with us."

Eden was puzzled. The alumni were still standing in

their places around the pool. They looked at each other uncertainly. It seemed this was not a part of their plan.

"Excuse me," Bola called from the diving board. "This is school property. You're not allowed here."

"Secret Service, ma'am," said one of them, flashing a badge in her direction. He and the other man still had Eden by the arms. "This way," he said to her.

"Stop," Bola commanded, scrambling frantically down the diving board's ladder. "This is unacceptable. You can't take her."

"Ma'am," the man said. He looked unimpressed. "We work for the president. We can do anything she wants."

They exited through a different door that led directly outside. Seeing the sun in the spotless blue sky was like reuniting with an old friend. Even though Eden had no clue where she was going, anywhere was better than in that pool.

A caravan of black vehicles that looked like elongated SUVs was lined up waiting. The men escorted her to one in the middle.

To her left, hundreds of students stood slack-jawed in shock. Eden supposed this was where they'd been directed for the fire drill.

"Sweden?" Mr. Willis said, approaching.

"Stay back, sir," said one of the Secret Service men.

The other one opened the door and gestured for her to get in.

"But—I'm soaking wet," she protested. She couldn't think of what else to say.

"Just get in," he said gruffly. And really, she didn't have any other options.

She climbed into the car's darkened interior and sat on a long seat that stretched the length of the car. As the man closed the door behind her, she saw that sitting across from her was a slender older woman with white hair and intelligent eyes.

She recognized the woman. But this time, not from the course guide.

"Please don't be afraid," the woman said. "I'm here to help you."

Eden blinked. "President Porter?"

The woman's wrinkles multiplied when she smiled.

"My dear," she said, "you can call me Faye."

Twenty-Two

"You were a *genie*," Eden said in wonder. The knowledge was nearly impossible to absorb. She could feel that the car had started moving, though little was visible through the dark tinted windows. She gazed at the president's—Faye's—genie bracelet on her aged, spot-speckled wrist.

"One of the few who wished for mortality," Faye said. "And of those, the only one still alive."

"And you're the *president* of the *United States*!" Eden squeezed some water from her braid. "Wait a second. You coming to San Diego is a big deal—I saw it on the news and everything. You didn't come—"

"For you? Of course I did." Faye watched amusedly as this sank in.

"But don't you have more important things to do?"

"More important than this? I don't think so."

Eden shook her head in amazement. "I can't believe

the president is an alum! Why wouldn't Xavier and Goldie tell me? You'd think they'd brag about you."

Now that she was close to Faye, Eden could detect traces of the young strawberry blonde from the course guide: the shape of her lips, the arch of her light eyebrows. And her eyes were just the same: piercing, but kind.

"I don't communicate with Xavier and Goldie," Faye said. "When I retired, I told them I wanted to leave that world behind me, and they've honored that. I'm sure they've kept up with my career, but they've never tried to contact me."

"I'm sure they have too. Xavier was at that UN summit you spoke at." Faye's eyebrows lifted subtly, and a pleased look crossed her face.

"But I thought all the genies who'd wished for mortality were long gone." Eden thought back to her last day of lessons, when she'd studied Faye's section in the course guide. "The last genie in the lamp before me was Cadence, and you were just before her. Right? You were the resident genie up until the start of the Second World War."

"That's right."

"Then how are you still alive? You would have been fifty when you left the lamp. You're not over a hundred mortal years old, are you?"

"You forget," Faye said gently, "there are no limits

for a genie's last wish. I didn't wish for mortal life continuing from the point of my retirement. I wished to be born into the world as a mortal, and age from that point forward."

Eden's heart surged with a sudden, desperate need for empathy. "Did you hate being a genie too?"

Something small and dear collapsed behind Faye's eyes, but it wasn't what Eden had hoped for.

"No," she said. "I loved my years in the lamp. When I was granting, I got to light up mortals' lives. That made me want to change the world for the better." She sighed. "Though I must say, it's been more difficult than I imagined."

Eden remembered the speech Bola had played on the TV. President Porter—Faye—had said you couldn't see the world's beauty until you brightened it. Who would have guessed it had all started with granting wishes!

In the pool, Eden had seen in vivid detail how a genie's power could be used to harm humanity. But Faye was on the opposite end of the spectrum: she was a perfect example of how much good could come of granting.

Eden felt like she'd been studying a painting for hours and just learned it was upside down. Maybe she'd been looking at her job all wrong.

"So now you're mortal," Eden said. "That means you're going to die?"

"Hopefully not for a while."

"But why would you choose that? Wouldn't you rather stay and light up Earth forever?"

"Life on Earth was designed to begin and to end. It's hard for a genie to see that from the lamp."

Eden stared at Faye's frail frame and sagging skin. Even though she looked older than the immortals, she was centuries younger than most of them. But while they had wasted centuries spent in bitterness or decadence, Faye had fought to make the world a better place.

Was that because she was mortal, or was it the other way around? What made a woman wise? What gave meaning to a life?

For some reason, tears blurred Eden's eyes. "I'm sorry," she said. "It's been a long couple of days."

"Don't be sorry. You're being very brave." Undeterred by the puddle forming under her, Faye moved to the seat beside Eden and wrapped an arm around her.

"What should I do?" Eden asked. "I'm not going to give the lamp to the Electric, but I don't know how to get them off my trail. And the Loyals are doing everything they can to try to convince me to go back."

Faye pursed her lips. "Are you ready to go back?"

"No," Eden said emphatically. "My heart is here. I'm not meant for the lamp."

"But even if you manage to evade the alumni, your time on Earth will inevitably end when the boy makes his other two wishes."

Eden squinted. "You know everything, huh?"

Faye smiled in answer.

"How?"

"I used to be a genie. *And* I'm president of the United States. I may be mortal, but I've got a few tricks up my sleeve."

Eden shook her head. "Anyway, Tyler's not going to use those wishes. He wants to keep me here on Earth." Warmth flowed from her head to her toes as she said it aloud.

Faye paused before replying.

"But while you're here, the world's wishes can't be granted."

It took a moment to register the pang of another betrayal.

"But you're not one of the Loyals," Eden insisted. "You just rescued me from them!"

"I took you away from them because I don't think you should be intimidated into going back to the lamp," Faye said. Then, more gently: "You should do it because it's right."

Eden's heart seared with pain. She'd never felt more alone.

"I know you believe you weren't meant for the lamp. But you're a genie. It's who you are. Before you can live here on Earth, you need to carry out your duties as a genie."

Everything in her wanted to argue, but this time Eden couldn't find the words.

Faye checked her cell phone. "The students have returned to classes. We'll drop you off at the end of the building closest to your locker. The door will be unlocked."

Eden wiped away another tear. "It isn't fair," she said—but even as she said it, she knew what the answer would be.

Faye smiled sadly as she spoke Xavier's words: "Life isn't fair, my darling."

The car had come to a stop. One of the Secret Service men opened the door and let the shocking sunlight in.

Just before Eden slid out of the seat, Faye placed her warm, wrinkled hands on her arm.

"You know," she said, "you're not like anyone else on Earth. Mortal *or* immortal. Don't forget that." She squeezed her arm softly. "Only you can make this decision. Now go, and make the right one."

The door was open, just like Faye had said. Eden stole down the silent hall, spun her locker's combination, grabbed the denim backpack, and ducked into the restroom.

Luckily, no one was inside. Eden stared at herself in the mirror. She was a mess—all damp and bedraggled. Her eyes were ringed with red. She unraveled her wet braid and tried to comb her fingers through it, but the pool's chlorine had made it stiff and sticky.

Images from her trip into Sylvana's grantings were pinging through her mind like pinballs. The Loyals were right: she *had* underestimated Sylvana. Knowing what she knew now, it was absurd to think she'd imagined they were just alike! Her own silly tricks on wishers were nothing compared to the horrors she'd witnessed.

And yet, her short exchange with Faye had hit her hardest. This time she respected the person who'd told her what she didn't want to hear. Maybe—maybe—that meant it was time to listen.

She unzipped the backpack and pulled out the lamp. Holding it in her hands, she considered.

What if she went back now? Maybe it *was* the right thing to do. Electra would lose any chance of getting the lamp, the Loyals would be satisfied, and everything would return to normal.

But wouldn't Tyler and Sasha be sad if she disappeared?

Wouldn't they wonder why she hadn't said goodbye?

One thing was certain: if she made the request for reentry, Tyler wouldn't get to make his other wishes. Those wishes could change the Rockwells' lives. After the trouble she'd caused, didn't she owe that much to them?

She slipped the lamp back into the backpack. Besides her notebook, there was one more thing inside—a stiff paper rectangle.

She couldn't help smiling when she saw what it was: the photo from the roller coaster. In it, she and Tyler were screaming with their hands in the air. They looked happier than mortals who'd just won the lottery's biggest prize. Even though it was the first photo she'd ever seen of herself, she knew that what it had captured didn't exist inside the lamp.

The girl in the photograph was Eden on Earth. The girl she was always meant to be.

"Here you are!"

Hurriedly Eden tucked the photo into her back pocket. Ms. Mattris was standing at the door. "We've been looking for you."

Eden cleared her throat. "I was just going back to class—"

"No, come with me," Ms. Mattris said. "Your mother's here."

"Well, she can turn around and leave. I'm not going with her."

"Actually, you have to." Eden's stomach dropped as Sylvana stepped into the bathroom. "You're no longer a student at this school."

Twenty-Three

Apparently, minors under eighteen years of age had zero rights in America. Sylvana had told Principal Willis that Eden would be returning to Sweden with her. Without any need for Eden's consent, she'd withdrawn her from Mission Beach Middle School.

They wouldn't even let her go into second period to talk to Sasha. "You'd disturb the class," Sylvana said, and Ms. Mattris agreed.

"What happened yesterday?" Sylvana demanded once they were outside. "I thought we were in this together."

She slipped her sunglasses on. Today's pair was a cat's-eye shape, to accentuate her cheekbones. Eden fought the urge to rip them off her face.

"What happened was, I discovered why you wanted me to come to Paris with you so badly."

"Once we get there, you'll realize it's where you belong," Sylvana said, trying to pull her toward the parking lot. Her red convertible was parked sideways across two handicapped spots. "More importantly, you belong with *me*."

Eden yanked her arm away. "Why would I go with you *now*? I'm not an idiot."

Sylvana set the sunglasses on top of her head. "What do you mean?"

"I know all about you, and Violet, and Electra. I understand what your whole plan was."

Sylvana's unearthly turquoise eyes seemed to glow even brighter. "Please, tell me."

"You want me to come with you so you can try to persuade me to take off the bracelet—which will allow you to take control of the lamp. *That's* your plan to 'end the reign of tyranny.'"

Sylvana stared at her for so long, Eden thought her eyes might burn holes straight through her. Suddenly, she let out a robust laugh. "You *are* a clever little genie!"

Eden watched her in utter repulsion. "How is that funny? Obviously I'm not going to go along with it. You've already lost."

"Oh, but that's where you're wrong!" Sylvana said. "I can guarantee that within the hour, you're going to do exactly what I want."

"You're legitimately crazy." Eden crossed her arms.

"There's no chance I'm even getting in that car with you."

Sylvana sighed. "You're only making things harder for yourself. You'll have no one else to blame when your little friends ask why you didn't help them."

Eden's body went ice-cold. "What are you talking about? Have you done something to Tyler or Sasha?"

"Oh, I wouldn't interrupt *them*. They're busy getting a splendid education, courtesy of the State of California. However, their father joined your aunt Violet for a little outing today. And things haven't gone the way he planned."

"He did *what*?"

Sylvana hopped in the convertible and started the ignition. "Why don't you come along and find out?"

"Tell me what you've done to Mr. Rockwell!"

"I'll tell you this," Sylvana snarled. "I can make one phone call and he's dead." She revved the engine. "Now get in."

Eden's nerves twisted up like pretzels as the convertible sped down a road that was becoming familiar. They drove along the coast until the tall structures of the amusement park came into view, and then, with a screech of tires, Sylvana swerved into the parking lot.

"Here we are," she said brightly. "Now, tell me this isn't more fun than school."

Eden glared at her.

"No? Personally, I love a good roller-coaster ride."

Two women were guarding the entrance. They didn't wear genie bracelets, but Eden recognized them from the course guide. One was Zoe, the second genie to ever reside in the lamp. The other was Julianna, the feisty-looking green-eyed genie who'd granted for mortals like Abigail Adams. They nodded to Sylvana as they passed.

Inside, the park was empty. The silence was a stark, eerie contrast to the laughter and screams of joy a day earlier. Even though it was 10 A.M. on a Tuesday, Eden had a feeling the vacancy was due to Zoe and Julianna, and not the time of day.

Sylvana glided through the park like she owned it. Eden followed, clutching the backpack in her arms.

They passed the bumper cars and the carousel, and still Eden saw no one. Finally they reached the Vertical Plunge, the ride that dropped mortals from high above. At its foot stood several more Electra employees: a stunning woman with caramel skin, a gaunt alum with deep purple hair, a golden-haired fairy-princess type, and Violet.

"Eden, meet Athena, Monroe, and Kingsley. And you know Violet."

Eden's skin prickled at the cruel curiosity in the women's faces. She swallowed. "Where's Mr. Rockwell?"

In answer, they all looked skyward. The Vertical Plunge's seat was at its highest height, a hundred feet above.

Squinting, Eden could see that there was one person in the seat. One person, and no safety harness protecting him.

"Is that him?" Eden screamed. "What did you *do*?"

"Sounds to me like you can see for yourself," Athena said.

"But he's not strapped in! He could fall!"

"That's the point," said Monroe. She smoothed her long purple locks with a bony white hand.

"Help!" Mr. Rockwell's voice drifted from above.

"Violet and I loved meeting him last night." Sylvana peered up at him. "We thought it would be fun to take him for a ride this morning."

"Mr. Rockwell, put the harness on!" Eden called, cupping her hands around her mouth.

"He can't. It's locked open."

Eden thought frantically. She remembered the cell phones they all carried. "He'll call for help! Police will be here any moment!"

But Violet grinned and held up a phone. "I don't think so. He let me 'borrow' this right before he climbed on."

"Let him down!" Eden demanded.

"Absolutely," Sylvana said. "What goes up, must

always come down. The question is *how*. In the seat, or out of it?" She leaned close and spoke low in Eden's ear. "Alive, or dead?"

Eden remembered her conversation with Tyler about the rides. He'd said mortals enjoyed the thrill of them because they were strapped in. That without the straps and brakes, they'd probably die.

Sylvana wasn't bluffing. If he fell from that height, he probably wouldn't survive.

"Take off the bracelet and hand over the lamp," said Monroe. "If you do, he'll walk away safe. Otherwise, your friends become orphans."

A sick, spinning sense of remorse washed over Eden. She should have known something like this would happen. She knew how desperate Sylvana was to get ahold of the lamp. Xavier and Goldie had warned her, and so had the Loyals. She'd even seen Sylvana's ruthlessness in action for herself. Why hadn't she listened?

Deep down, she knew why: because she'd wanted so badly to stay on Earth. And now, as a result, her only friends might lose their second parent.

"It's easy to save him," said Kingsley, the one who looked like a fairy princess. "Just take off the bracelet and give us the lamp."

If she did, she'd save Mr. Rockwell but sacrifice Xavier and Goldie. It was either her masters, or Sasha and Tyler's dad. There was no way to win.

"Might as well go ahead and hand it over," said Violet, folding her arms. "One way or another, we're going to get it."

Eden glared at her. All this had started with Violet on the beach. She wished with all her being that their paths had never crossed.

"I'll never let you hurt Xavier and Goldie," Eden said.

"Ew," Sylvana said, disgusted. "You sound like one of *them*."

"One of *us*?" Eden recognized the voice, but she had to see its owner to believe it was really her. Sure enough, when she whipped around she saw Bola, magenta lipstick freshly applied, skin gleaming in the sun. Flanking her were two pairs of Loyals, each holding one of the Electric guards from the gate. The other genies who'd surrounded the pool formed a fuming mass behind her.

Eden took the opportunity to scoot aside so Sylvana could face her adversary.

"Bola," Sylvana said. "It's been a long time."

"Centuries," Bola said coldly.

"You haven't changed a bit."

"Why would I?"

And with that, the pleasantries were over.

"Release my employees," Sylvana commanded.

Bola held her gaze for a moment before nodding to

her underlings. Zoe and Julianna joined their Electric compatriots. The two alumni armies faced one another.

"How did you know we were here?" Sylvana demanded.

"I saw you driving away with Eden through the window in my classroom," Bola said. She eyed Eden. "I didn't think Faye would be so quick to release you."

"You were with Faye?" Violet asked in wonder.

"Her Secret Service interrupted our trip down memory lane," Bola said dryly. "Anyway, naturally I had to follow you."

"And when she left, I left," came a new voice. It was Sasha, coming toward them with Tyler beside her. Ms. Mattris was behind them, looking terrified. "I knew something was up when she left in the middle of the lesson. I pulled Tyler out of Pre-Algebra and convinced Ms. Mattris to drive us. We followed Bola's car—and the others that joined along the way."

Ms. Mattris shook her head. "I'm so confused. Are you all from Sweden?"

Bola looked at her with pity. "Ms. Mattris, why don't you go back to your car?"

Wide-eyed, Ms. Mattris nodded. Wobbling on her heels, she staggered in the direction of the park's entrance. Eden hoped she had an emergency stash of chocolate to soothe her nerves.

Seeing Sasha and Tyler filled Eden's heart to the

brim, but her pulse was pounding. They had no idea what they'd walked into.

"Why are we here, anyway?" Tyler asked.

"And why did you get in the car with the president?" Sasha added. "And why are you *wet*?"

"*Tyler!*" Mr. Rockwell called. His voice was faint and faraway. "*Sasha!*"

"Where did that come from?" Sasha asked, looking around frantically. "It sounded like Dad."

"Look up, sweetheart," Sylvana said slyly.

There was a pause as everyone did exactly that.

"*Dad!*" Sasha screamed.

"Wow." Bola shook her head. "Sylvana, you've out-done yourself. You have one cold immortal heart."

"Anything for justice," Sylvana snarled. She turned and spoke to the Rockwells sweetly. "All your friend Eden has to do is take off her bracelet and give us the lamp, and then we'll lower him to safety. Kids, don't you want her to do that?"

"Eden," Bola thundered, "do *not listen*."

Eden squeezed the backpack more tightly, feeling the lamp's shape. "I'm not going to."

"In that case, you better hold on up there!" Sylvana called.

"You wouldn't," said Bola.

"Oh, really? Athena, show them we're serious." At the base of the ride, Athena pulled a lever. Feeling like she was in the middle of a nightmare, Eden watched the seat drop.

But the fall was a short one. Sasha screamed, and Mr. Rockwell cried out in terror—but he stayed in the seat. Squinting, Eden could see he was clinging to the unlatched safety harness.

"Does that make things clearer?" Sylvana asked.

Ivy stepped out from behind Bola. "Eden, you can still make the request for reentry," she implored. "You'll go back to the lamp, no harm done. Everyone will be safe."

"Are you kidding?" Sylvana scoffed. "If you do that, we'll *definitely* kill him. Probably them too," she said, indicating Tyler and Sasha.

"Better them than our masters," Bola hissed.

"Your *masters* are liars and oppressors!"

The Loyals gasped. "How *dare* you!" said Genevieve.

As the bickering escalated, heat crept up Eden's neck. How had it come to this? The women stood in pairs or small groups, screaming at each other. Some of them had even started clawing and hitting one another. They were brutal soldiers on an amusement park battlefield, beautiful on the outside, but heartless on the inside.

You're a genie, Faye had said. *It's who you are.* It was the same thing Goldie had always told her. As much as Eden wanted to change that, maybe the truth was that she couldn't.

Sighing, she glanced at her genie bracelet. And suddenly, she remembered who she was—and why it mattered.

Eden looked at her friends. Sasha was weeping; Tyler stood still as stone, frowning at the top of the Vertical Plunge.

The Loyals and the Electric were busy fighting. For the moment, they'd forgotten all about Eden.

"Tyler," she murmured, careful not to attract their attention, "you have to make your last two wishes."

"No," he said. "We can't go down without a fight."

"We don't want you to leave," Sasha said through tears.

"They *will* kill him. Do you understand that? And it won't stop, even then. Neither side will stop until they get what they want." She blinked back her own tears. "I'm a genie. I may not like it, but it's who I am." She took a breath. "You have to wish to save your dad. And I have to go back where I belong."

Sasha grabbed her and hugged her tightly. A hot tear dropped onto Eden's shoulder.

When they parted, she faced Tyler. It was hard to look him in the eye. A day earlier, here in this park, she'd hoped against hope that his wish might change her destiny. How differently things had turned out.

He raised a hand and gently tugged a lock of her hair, still damp from the pool. "I really, really wanted you to stay," he said. He looked away, and his jaw muscle tensed—just like it had when she'd denied his second wish.

"Will we ever see you again?" Sasha asked.

Eden focused on this moment, mentally storing it to treasure when she was alone again. She wanted to remember them like this. The freckles sprinkled across their faces, the earnest look in their eyes. Her friends.

"You never know, do you?" she said.

"Okay. I'm ready to make my second wish." Tyler leaned in and whispered so only she could hear. "I wish you could see how special you are."

The instant the sentence ended, the park seemed to freeze. The wisher and the lamp were in accord. He'd triggered the magic that made wishes come true. She couldn't have denied it if she'd wanted to.

The snap of her fingers was a reflex—as inevitable as breathing.

At first there was a sense of floating straight off the ground. The joy inside her was like helium in a balloon. All the burdens, worries, and fears she'd accumulated on Earth lifted off her shoulders. Her brain rang with soaring revelation: she *was* special.

Love was coursing like a current through her veins. Love for *everything*: not just easy-to-love things, like sunshine and dogs and carrot cake, but for the whole wide world and all the mortals who lived there. Not only

Sasha and Tyler and Mr. Rockwell, but also Skye and Claire, the man with the 'hawk, Darryl Dolan, Mr. Willis.

She was overwhelmed, too, by love for the life she'd lived. The hours of lessons, the big marble globe, her beautiful bedroom, the comfort she'd grown up with in the lamp her masters called paradise. And, finally, for her family. Because for the first time she saw clearly that they *were* her family. It didn't matter that Goldie hadn't given birth to her or that she looked nothing like Xavier. They loved her the way Tyler and Sasha loved Mr. Rockwell. The way they'd once loved their mom.

As her euphoria swelled, Eden forgot all about the genies and loosened her grip on the backpack. She was jolted abruptly back to reality when Violet yanked it from her hands.

Once the lamp was up for grabs, all hell broke loose. The genies piled on Violet like starving mortals desperate for the world's last piece of food.

"You'd better hurry," Eden said. In spite of the madness, she felt quite calm.

"I hope you're not thinking of doing something stupid," Sylvana screeched as she emerged from the pileup. For the first time, she was in a state of disarray. One strap of her tank top had fallen, random chunks of hair were pulled loose from her ponytail, and only one-half of her sunglasses sat precariously on her head. She moved to the lever at the bottom of the Vertical Plunge. "His life is in my hands!"

"That's about to change," Sasha growled. "Tyler, go."

Tyler closed his eyes, and for a moment all was still.

"I wish for my family to be safe—and stronger than ever before."

At the very same moment Sylvana pulled the lever, Eden raised her hand and snapped.

But it was too late for Sylvana to hurt them anymore. Eden's bracelet glowed bright as Tyler's wish was instantly granted.

As the alumni continued to struggle, the lamp vanished from their reach—and so did the genie who lived inside.

Twenty-Four

Eden reentered through the study, as always. But this time, the masters of the lamp weren't waiting sternly at their desks. They practically threw themselves on her.

"Thank God!" Xavier said.

"You're home!" Goldie's voice rang out.

All at once, they were crying, all three. Goldie sobbed passionately, and even Xavier's eyes were wet with tears.

When they finally let go, she got a good look at them. They wore their anguish like funeral garb. In addition to his mustache, Xavier was sporting at least a day's growth of facial hair. His teary eyes were puffy with exhaustion. Goldie's chest heaved and her cheeks glowed pink with emotion. They were, both of them, a mess.

Over me? Eden thought in wonder. But then, she knew the answer. Yes, over her. After all, they were her family.

"Are you all right?" Xavier sputtered. He ran his hands over her hair and squeezed her shoulders, as if making sure all of her was there.

"What *happened*?" Goldie begged. "Sweet girl, were you hurt out there?"

Something crumpled in Eden's chest, and her tears flowed afresh.

"We couldn't see," said Xavier frantically. "At the end, it was so hard to tell what happened."

Eden smiled through the pain.

"I'm okay," she said. "Everything's going to be okay."

For the next few hours, they talked as much as they could talk and then some. Sitting around the dining room table, they devoured a freshly baked carrot cake as Eden told them everything.

She started with her rescue from the ocean, then moved on to school, the hot air balloon, and the journey into Sylvana's grantings. Goldie and Xavier listened absorbedly, desiring endless details as she filled in the gaps between the parts they'd seen and heard through the telescope. All of it spilled out, even the parts she knew would get her in trouble.

As she spoke, Xavier watched her with a sad affection she'd never seen in him before. It struck her that in the past few days, he'd changed too.

When she reached the end of her story—the

showdown at the amusement park, and Tyler's final two wishes—her eyes filled with tears again.

"I'm grateful it happened," she said. "I'd wanted to live in the world for so long. But I'm sorry—so sorry— because I put you in danger. I know I must have hurt you. I understand now that you've loved me all along. My whole life, you've given me everything I need."

"Oh, darling!" Goldie covered her mouth with a hand.

The flames of the candles on the table danced in the dark.

There was a tilting, shifting moment before Xavier cleared his throat. "You did disobey me."

"I know," Eden said quietly.

"Repeatedly, when you consider the messages."

She hung her head. "I know. And I deserve what- ever punishment you give me."

He winced. "We'll discuss that later. For now, we're glad you're home."

Eden smiled weakly. "Me too," she said in a husky half-voice. Drawing a shaky breath, she pushed her empty plate away. "Would it be okay for me to go to bed now?"

With all her heart, Eden wanted to want to be exactly where she was: in her bedroom in the lamp, with the family she'd discovered she loved so much, patiently awaiting her next opportunity to light up a mortal's life with a granting.

She wanted to want to. But that didn't mean she wanted to.

Propped on the pillows on her canopy bed, she gazed around the genie's chambers. The room that had so recently contained her whole life was now a museum of her childhood. The frozen chandelier. The spacious closet. Inside it, beneath the sumptuous clothes, the rose lipstick marks numbering her outings.

Even the scent of the air was familiar: that perfume of innocence, ignorance, and comfort.

In a way, it was nice to be home. And yet, spending thousands of nights to come here seemed unthinkable. How could she readjust to not having mortals her age to talk to? To candlelight, recycled air, and sitting in one classroom all day long?

It wasn't that she was ungrateful. Tyler's wish truly had made her realize how special it was to be a genie— to be *Eden*.

But she couldn't deny that Earth had changed her too. She'd seen, felt, and learned things she couldn't in the lamp. Frankly, she supposed, she'd grown up.

Earth had exposed her to all the things Xavier and Goldie had tried to protect her from. She understood now why Xavier had warned her about cars and bodies of water. She'd seen how a mortal's death could break the hearts of those still living. She'd experienced the gut-wrenching feeling that came from being told you don't belong.

She'd learned about the dark, angry mission of Electra, and witnessed Sylvana's wicked ways.

They'd wanted to keep her safe and innocent. And in the lamp's sheltered confines, she *was*.

And yet, when she remembered the smell of the ocean, the thrill of standing in a basket as it rose into the air, the satisfaction of shared laughter—she was brutally, violently heartsick.

She went to the closet to change into a nightgown. She was still wearing Sasha's shorts and tank top. But as she slipped the shorts over her hips, something sharp poked through the fabric. She reached in the pocket and pulled out the photograph from the roller coaster. There she was again, shiny and sure, beaming with the joy of exploring the world.

Eden on Earth. The girl she could never be. Her heart swelled with pain.

"Eden?" Goldie said as she knocked on the door. Eden rebuttoned her shorts and went to it.

Goldie brimmed with nervous energy like a boiling teakettle. "Xavier and I want to speak with you. Come to the study, dear."

She bustled down the spiral stairs, and Eden followed closely behind. What now? Had Xavier settled on the terms of her punishment? Of course it was only a matter of time.

As they entered, Eden thought about the night when she'd made her escape. She'd slipped the drawers from their places to find the forbidden ladder that would lead her to freedom—or at least, where she'd thought she'd find freedom. Remembering, she was shocked by her own boldness.

Somehow, the study seemed even larger and more impressive post-Earth. It was like a throne room, replete with a certain majesty. Xavier was standing in front of the telescope. Goldie joined him there, and they stood hand in hand, strong as a fortress, united and equal.

"What's going on?" Eden asked apprehensively.

They looked at one another, and Goldie nodded. Xavier spoke with gravity. "Eden," he said, "your time in the lamp is over."

She nearly choked. She'd dreamed about leaving the lamp for as long as she could remember, but hearing his words made her indignant.

"What do you mean?" she cried.

Xavier swallowed. Eden saw Goldie squeeze his hand.

"That can't be! The rules say a genie has to live in the lamp until she's granted nine hundred and ninety-nine wishes!"

"Sometimes," Xavier said, "rules change."

Her heart was racing. "I don't understand."

Goldie met her eyes. "You're still going to be a genie, dear. You've got a lot of wishes to go."

"And the lamp will still circulate Earth, just like it always has," Xavier said. "But you'll no longer be bound to it—at least, not in the same way." He raised his eyebrows. "Do you understand? You're going to live out there."

Over the past few days Eden had seen and heard a few bombshells—but this one trumped them all.

She'd thought things could only be different if she rebelled against the system. She'd never dared to dream that she might have the power to change it.

"Your duties as a genie haven't changed," Xavier went on. "When a wisher rubs the lamp, you'll still be summoned. You'll just be on Earth between grantings, instead of here, inside the lamp."

"But—where will I stay?" Eden gasped.

"You'll meet your new guardian when you arrive," Xavier said. "Goldie and I are still your masters, but she'll look after you while you're on Earth."

"She's lovely," Goldie said. Eden could see she was trying her very best not to cry.

"Will I still see you?"

"One of us will come to Earth for your post-granting assessments," said Xavier. "And of course, we'll visit you. But one at a time."

"But the lamp," Eden protested. "It won't allow me to live out there—will it?"

"Goldie and I designed the lamp," Xavier said. "Even for us, some of its rules are unchangeable. But in this case"—he shrugged—"change has to happen."

"What about the bracelet's power? Won't it keep the lamp wherever I am?"

Goldie and Xavier exchanged a glance.

"Considering the circumstances," he said, "it seems that in order to best protect both you and the lamp, the bracelet's powers must be altered. Your genie bracelet will still be active, but your connection to the lamp will cease to exist the way you know it."

She frowned. "You're not kicking me out, are you?"

Goldie laughed through her tears. "Of course not! Do you have any idea how much we love you?"

"That's how we know this is right." There was pain in Xavier's eyes, but Eden could see that he finally understood her.

"I always said you weren't meant for that world," he said. "I was wrong. You weren't meant for ours."

And it was true. She'd known all along—since her earliest lessons about waterfalls, jungles, and trains. Since the granting in France when she'd first felt the sun. Every time she'd added three more lipstick ticks to the tally in her closet.

Still, fear took its best aim at her. Images from her

journey into Sylvana's grantings grasped at her mind. The veil of darkness the alumni had tried to pull over her threatened to obscure her vision.

But then there was a still, small voice in her ear. It said:

There is *pain on Earth. But it's worth it anyway.*

And she knew she could never look back.

"Okay then." Eden lifted her chin. "I'm ready."

She hugged Goldie first, taking care to store the memory of her fragrance deep in her brain. "I'll see you soon, my dear," said Goldie tenderly.

"Goldie, you *hate* Earth," Eden said with dismay. "You haven't been there for thousands of years!"

Goldie wiped away the tears that spilled onto her full pink cheeks. "I'd say you're well worth a trip."

Next was Xavier. He wrapped his arms around Eden, then pulled back and gripped her shoulders.

"You're still a genie," he said intently. "Graceful. Brilliant. And *terribly* beautiful. Don't let the world tell you anything different."

She blinked back tears. Looking straight into his eyes, she nodded. "I think I finally know what you mean."

She took a deep breath. Even though she knew what she was doing was right, she had no idea what might come next.

But wasn't that part of the adventure?

So she held out her hand and snapped her fingers. And just like that, she was gone.

Gone to love, disappointment, and elation. To trees and windows, birds and sand. To photos and friends and hot air balloons. To that dizzy sweet moment at the top of the roller coaster, just before the drop—

Yes, Eden was gone.

And then—she arrived.